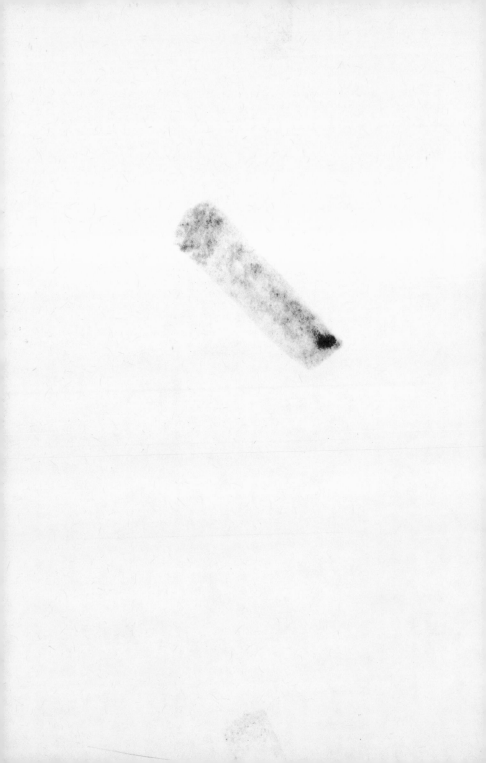

Rusty Timmons'
First Million

Joan Carris

RUSTY TIMMONS' FIRST MILLION

Illustrated by Kim Mulkey

J. B. LIPPINCOTT

NEW YORK

Library of Congress Cataloging in Publication Data
Carris, Joan Davenport.
    Rusty Timmons' first million.

    Summary: Hoping that his awesome moneymaking scheme,
a summer youth employment service, will help win back
his old friend Dan, seventh grader Rusty finds instead
that it leads to an unexpected new friendship with bossy
Ruthann Miller.
    [1. Business enterprises—Fiction. 2. Moneymaking
projects—Fiction. 3. Summer employment—Fiction.
4. Friendship—Fiction] I. Mulkey, Kim, ill. II. Title.
PZ7.C2347Ru 1985   [Fic]   85-40096
ISBN 0-397-32154-6
ISBN 0-397-32155-4 (lib. bdg.)

1 2 3 4 5 6 7 8 9 10
First Edition

*To my readers, who understand
the value of friendship*

Contents

Rusty Timmons' First Million

1

Vacation on the Way

Rusty joggled the pages of his science report up and down on his desk, trying to get them into a neat pile, making a racket in the quiet classroom. Mr. Ingram, the seventh-grade science teacher, frowned at Rusty with his familiar you-know-better-than-that face.

Rusty winked at Mr. Ingram and pointed to the report on his desk. "Great paper. You're going to love it," he whispered.

Mr. Ingram whispered back, "I'll love it better if you get rid of all the grammatical errors. This is Wednesday, remember, and the final copy's due Friday. Don't fall apart the last week of school, Russell." He smiled briefly before turning his attention to the papers on his own desk.

Last week of school. Rusty was ready to be finished with seventh grade. He had great hopes for summer and his odd-job business.

"Hey, Rusty," hissed a low voice behind him. Rusty looked over his shoulder at Bob Matthews.

"Ball game. Bottom of Holly Tree Court," Bob whispered. "After school."

Rusty shook his head. "I've got a job today."

"Again?" Bob's voice squeaked.

"Gentlemen!" Mr. Ingram's tone caused all twenty-four heads to jerk to attention. "Work on your papers, please. Now!"

"Yessir," Rusty and Bob said together. Rusty flushed with embarrassment as all eyes looked their way. He hated it when he blushed glow-pink underneath his flaming red hair. He felt like a living red light.

"Hey, Ketchup," teased a low voice only two desks away.

Rusty gritted his teeth and refused to look at her. Ruthann Miller had been calling him Ketchup since kindergarten. She had a name for everybody.

With determination, Rusty concentrated on his paper. Dolphins were a terrific topic. Bright, smiling creatures without care. Or so they appeared to him. Rusty felt a kinship with them that he hoped would show in his report and help to earn him a better grade.

Out of the corner of his eye, Rusty saw Dan Brower slip a note to the new girl. Dan was clever about notes and rarely got caught. Over the years, Rusty had gotten zillions of notes from him.

Recently, though, all Dan's notes had gone to her. Tiffany Smeltzer. She was from New York City, and no one had any idea why her family had moved to a small town in southern Ohio just four months ago. Rusty often asked himself what Hampshire could possibly offer to a girl like Tiffany.

He watched as she glanced over her shoulder and smiled at Dan. Dan grinned back, then pretended to be examining his science report. He poised a pen over the papers on his desk and looked profoundly absorbed.

He looks *older*, Rusty thought, realizing for the first time that Dan had shot past him in more than height. Rusty leaned forward to get a good look at Dan's upper lip. Was that the beginning of a mustache? Nah! Everybody had a little hair on his upper lip. Rusty stroked the pale red-gold hairs above his own lip. Yeah, they were still there. Not growing, though, or anything interesting like that.

Dan shifted in his seat and stretched his legs out into the aisle. His legs were long and hard, muscled like the rest of him. Surreptitiously, Rusty felt the friendly little roll that protruded above his jeans. "Just baby fat. You'll be shooting up any day now." That's what the doctor had promised at his last checkup.

Still, Rusty was beginning to resent being shorter and rounder than Dan. They had always done everything together, so why weren't they growing up together?

He looked down at his report and noticed a bit of folded paper sticking out from the edge of it. He checked to see that Mr. Ingram was hard at work before he unfolded the note.

"Party at my house Thursday night, 7:30. Bring food. Debbie." Rusty crumpled the note and stuck it in his pocket before he looked over to his right. Debbie was smiling expectantly at him, and he nodded to her as he made an okay sign down low, beside his seat, where only she could see.

Rusty checked his watch, then the wall clock. He was sick of sitting at a desk all day, and ready for a good party. He wondered if Debbie had invited all forty-eight in the seventh grade or just some. He didn't think she liked the new girl. Tiffany had been friendly, but reserved and awfully quiet in school. She wasn't like the Hampshire girls. He was sure of that.

When the bell finally rang, Rusty shot out of his desk and down the hall to his locker. He took his math book, and his dolphin report for his mother to check before he rewrote it in ink.

"I think everybody's coming. Bring lots of food." Debbie stopped by his locker and shifted the load of books in her arms. "Can you get Julia to make brownies?"

Rusty's older sister, a junior in high school, had always made brownies whenever Rusty had a party. "I'll try," he said, "but she's got exams, so I can't promise."

"You'll talk her into it," Debbie replied confidently. "Are you coming to the Court for the game?" She had been a whirlwind shortstop since fifth grade, and a regular player for their pickup ball games. Usually, Rusty played catcher.

Today he shook his head. "I'm walking dogs again. It's the best of my jobs. Pays a dollar a day, and Mrs. Wayland's waiting for me right now."

Debbie made a face. "Boo. Why can't they wait till five-thirty?" Her blond ponytail bobbed back and forth as she talked.

"Got to keep the customers happy. Besides, when I'm rich and driving a car, you can say you knew me *when*." Rusty flashed a smile at Debbie.

She cocked her head to one side. "Okay then. See you tomorrow."

Rusty hurried across the hall and out the school door just in time to see Dan and Tiffany disappearing down the sidewalk ahead of him. Together again. Tiffany's long dark hair swung to and fro gracefully as she kept in step with Dan's long strides.

"She has everything!" Dan had told him weeks ago. "I mean, you wouldn't believe it! There's this giant game room with billiards, and an air hockey table, and Ping-Pong. They've got a video recorder and tons of movies, not ones they rent, but movies they *own*. And an instant movie camera so you can make a movie, then show it right away. She's getting a horse this spring—a palomino—and we thought of this great name for it: Champagne. Isn't that cool? We're fixing up the barn right now. You know, knocking out walls to make a big stall and getting the hay and straw? All that stuff. You wouldn't believe it!"

Rusty believed it. Tiffany's parents had bought the old McFarland place just a few blocks from school. It was the largest and most expensive property in Hampshire, although the house and its many outbuildings had sat empty for two years. Any idiot could see that money would be needed to bring the place back to life. Just as anyone could see from Tiffany's clothes and real leather notebooks that she was wealthy.

And she's pretty, Rusty admitted, thinking of her big dark eyes and abundant hair. He shook himself and set off for the Waylands' house. He didn't like to think about how much he missed Dan. Besides, he and Dan had too many good memories, too much friendship, for anyone to interfere for long. Of course, it would be great if *he* had something special at *his* place that made Dan want to come over more often.

"Take them to the park today," Mrs. Wayland told him as she handed over Duke's and Cocoa's leashes. "Duke needs to run, and Cocoa can keep up if she has to."

The rangy German shepherd and the brown poodle strained forward, pulling Rusty down the sidewalk. They yanked him on up Grove and out Parkview, as if they knew today was park day. Rusty panted after them. If he ran like Duke and Cocoa every day, he might lose that little roll around his waist.

Much later, as he slid into his seat at the supper table, he knew what would happen.

FWEEEEP! FWEEEEP! The whistle shattered the air. It was the loudest whistle made, and Rusty's seven-year-old sister, Mike, wore it all the time, blowing it whenever she felt the need.

"Michelle, not at the table!" Rusty's mother scolded.

"So there!" Rusty made a ha-ha face at Mike. "I was working!"

Mr. Timmons said, "Another day, another dollar, right?"

"Yup. And Dad, I know what I want to buy with my money. I thought of it this afternoon while I was walking the dogs. A basketball court. A full-size one with a metal pole, like at school. Dan loves basketball. We could have games all the time, right here."

"I haven't seen Dan lately. Seems like he was always here, especially on lasagna nights." Mrs. Timmons looked questioningly at Rusty.

"Yeah. He's, uh, he's been busy," Rusty said, not wanting his parents to probe too deeply. "Anyway, what do you think about the basketball idea, Dad? I can pay half. How much would one cost?"

"They're not cheap, Russ. Pole, backboard, cement base and slab. Probably three hundred dollars or more." Mr. Timmons helped himself to a second square of lasagna.

"Cripes! All I've earned in over a month is twenty-one dollars!"

"You don't need a basketball court," Mrs. Timmons said briskly. "Not when the school has four of them. Michelle, use your fork for the peas, not your fingers."

"It'll be warm enough to swim in the pool any day now," Julia suggested. "Dan always liked that, didn't he?"

Rusty shot a warning look at his older sister. He wondered if she could read minds. The pool wasn't good enough. They'd had it for three years and it wasn't exciting anymore.

"Russ, if you want a home basketball court, you'll have to pay for it yourself. Julia starts college in just over a year, and that tuition will really stretch our budget." Mr. Timmons reached over and squeezed Rusty's shoulder. "And you're next. You want four years of college, don't you?"

Rusty nodded and tried to smile at his father. "Yeah, I understand." And he did. But it didn't mean that there would be no basketball court. The more he thought about the great games they could have, the more he liked the idea. Dan was a super basketball player. Somehow, Rusty would have to find a way to earn three hundred dollars.

Julia pushed her chair back. "Exams are a pain. I have two to study for tonight. Disgusting." Her attractive face wrinkled in a frown. She pulled a rubber band from her pocket and twisted it around her long, reddish-brown hair to pull it out of her way. "On with it," she groaned, standing up.

"You don't want to study all night," Rusty said to her. "Wouldn't you like a little break in the middle?"

"That depends," Julia said, grinning at him. "I smell a con."

"No, no," he protested. "Just the truth. Do you know you're the most famous cook in school? My whole class thinks you're the best cook who ever lived."

"Come on, Rusty. Isn't that a bit thick?"

"No way! Your brownies are famous. Everybody in my class has asked for the recipe. I tell them it's a secret, but they never stop asking. That's fame."

"Uh-huh. I'm thrilled to death. I suppose you want me to make brownies tonight when I have to study for exams."

"Pleeeeeease, Julia. It's for a class party and I'll help. I'll chop nuts or sift flour. Whatever you want. And *I'll* wait around and take them out of the oven."

Julia closed her eyes. "I know I'm being conned." She opened her eyes again. "You promise you'll help?"

"Promise. I'll even owe you one. A favor anytime."

"Deal. Meet me here in the kitchen at eight-thirty. If you don't show, no brownies." Julia marched off down the hall.

"How about the cleanup?" Mrs. Timmons called after her.

Julia turned. "Right. But he owes me one. Dishes, Rusty."

"Okay. Mike, why don't you help clear the table?"

"FWEEEEEP!" answered Mike.

"Oh, Michelle," said her mother, sighing. She took off her glasses and pushed back a lock of the red, red hair she had passed on to Mike and Rusty. "I wish to goodness Uncle Wally hadn't given you that whistle."

Mike screwed up her face. "Uncle Wally knew I needed it 'cause I'm the littlest!"

"Second grade isn't so little," Rusty said, hoping for more help with the dishes.

"Not till next fall," Mike snapped. As far as Rusty and Julia could see, Mike had been spoiled ever since she had been frighteningly ill as a newborn.

"Michelle, *really*." Mrs. Timmons put her glasses back on. "You're old enough to help. Hop to it now while I work on my article for the paper. Toodle-oo, troops."

"Fweeeep," breathed the whistle in defeat. Mike tucked the shining bit of metal into her shirt and carried one clean knife back to the silverware drawer.

"Don't strain yourself," Rusty observed. He went to work, thoughts of the math final bugging him. He'd done well in math all year, but who knew what he'd forgotten since last fall? It was an uncomfortable thought, so Rusty pushed it away. Didn't he have a fantastic, mind-blowing report on dolphins? Anyway, as soon as he finished cleaning up supper, he would leaf through the math book just to be safe.

When Julia came into the kitchen at eight-thirty, Rusty was still reading his math book. "Are you going to tear up that test tomorrow?" she asked.

"You bet. I remember most of this stuff." He shut the book. "What should I do first, grease the pan?"

"Mmhm. You could learn to make brownies yourself, you know. It's easy." She began ladling flour into a measuring cup.

"Yeah," Rusty agreed. "Dan and I used to make the most terrific cinnamon things for breakfasts at camp. Out of biscuit mix, I think. Then we rolled them in butter and cinnamon sugar."

Julia stopped measuring flour. "Where is Dan anyway? I haven't seen him around in weeks."

"Well . . ." Rusty began awkwardly.

"You guys have a fight?"

"Nothing like that. He just . . . well, see . . . there's this new kid in our class." His mind flashed an image of Tiffany, black hair swirling round her face.

"What's his name?"

"It's a her. Tiffany."

"Tiffany? You gotta be kidding!"

Glumly, Rusty shook his head. "She's from New York City. Her family bought the old McFarland place."

"I heard that place cost a fortune, but it's a mess. They'll need dozens of workers to fix it up, I bet." Julia shook her head knowingly. As manager of the high school Youth Employment Service, she knew how hard it could be to find people for jobs like housecleaning and yard work. Rusty knew she would be glad of the summer break from managing the service.

"Tiffany's folks must be loaded," Julia concluded.

"You name it, they've got it. Dan said she's

getting a horse, so now they're fixing up the barn."

Julia poured flour into the sifter and began squeezing the sifter handle. "Money talks," she said crisply. "You've got lots of other friends. More than most kids. Forget him."

"I don't want to! We've been friends forever!" Rusty blurted without thinking.

"I'm sorry." Julia's voice was gentle. "Have you talked to Mom or Dad about it? We didn't know what was going on."

"It's okay—and I don't want to talk about it, especially not with the folks." Rusty's chin was high. "Mom'd just call his mom or something, like I was four years old. I'll work it out. Just don't say anything, all right?" Rusty's hazel eyes fixed on Julia's dark-brown ones.

"Okay by me, if that's what you want."

"Good. Anyway, as soon as I get my basketball court there won't be a problem. Dan loves basketball, and I'm getting to be a better guard all the time. Forwards aren't the whole game, you know. Where'd they be without the guards?"

Julia tipped her head to one side. "Rusty, I don't want to hurt your feelings, but have you thought about what you're saying?"

"Well . . ."

"You don't buy friends like that. With things."

"I'm not! Soon as he comes over and we get to messing around, he'll remember what fun we always had. It'll be like old times, see? And I'm a lot of fun. I'm a great guy." He smiled at her and shrugged. "Aren't I?"

"You're crazy." Julia laughed and poked him in the stomach.

Rusty dodged away. "Leave the spare tire alone. It's digesting lasagna."

"Come on, Rusty. Chop the nuts while I melt the margarine." She turned, looking at him over the door of the refrigerator. "If I can help with the basketball court, let me know. Anything short of money, that is."

"But that's what I'm short of—money." He was about to explain how much trouble he'd had lining up jobs when the telephone rang.

"Get that, Rusty. If it's Greg, tell him I'll call back. I have to finish these danged brownies."

"Hello?" Rusty said into the phone receiver.

"That you, Ketchup?"

It had to be Ruthann. The Mouth, he thought. "It's me. And you know I hate that name."

"That's why I use it. You're cute when you're

mad," Ruthann replied sweetly. Too sweetly.

"What do you want?"

"How much math are we supposed to review? Do we have to know all those formulas from way last October?"

"Every single formula. Good luck," Rusty sang out. "If you don't know it now, it's probably hopeless."

"Hah! I'm staying up to watch *Bride of Frankenstein.* I've got plenty of time. See you at the test."

"Geez!" Rusty exploded as he hung up the phone. "Ruthann's going to watch a horror movie while she studies math. And she'll probably get a higher grade than I will!"

Julia nodded. "She's a tough cookie. I hear her mom's still in Cincinnati. She ever come home anymore?"

"Who knows? Ruthann doesn't talk about her, and I've never even seen her. I heard her father left when she was a baby, so their gramma moved in with them. Then her mom left."

"Rough," Julia said slowly. "Well, I have to get back to work. Dump those nuts in the batter, Rusty, and stir 'em around. Then it's ready for the oven."

He thanked her and took over the baking.
While the brownies were in the oven, he and his
mother could check the dolphin report. And he
could think about how to raise three hundred
dollars.

2

Hidden in a Dream

Rusty put his science report in his room on the table that served as combination desk and model-building center. His mother had found spelling errors and a few dozen missing commas, but other than that she'd agreed that it was a knockout paper. He had copied it in ink and tomorrow he'd turn it in a day early.

Before he went to sleep, Rusty put the dollar he'd earned for walking Mrs. Wayland's dogs into his small, steel-blue safe with the combination lock. Now the safe held twenty-two dollars. Big whup. As he drifted toward sleep, Rusty admitted that his odd-job business might earn three hundred dollars—by the time he was twenty-two. Disgusted, he pulled the pillow over his head and dozed off.

Flat on his stomach, pillow over his head, Rusty didn't sleep well. He thrashed his legs uneasily, and mumbled about good ideas and bad ideas and three hundred dollars.

"I tell you we have to have more business or this entire company is going down the drain!" He pounded the desk with his fist.

"Yes, sir, Mr. Timmons, sir," quaked a thin man wearing a bilious green tie and a nervous expression. "I have a possible new sales manager for you to interview. New blood, sir. What do you say to that idea?" The thin man was still quaking.

"Well, trot someone in here then." He pointed toward the polished-wood door. On it a sign said, RUSSELL WAYNE TIMMONS, PRESIDENT. "And hurry up about it!"

"Yessir." The quaker scurried out the door and scurried right back in, trailing a tall slim woman in a navy-blue suit. Her hair was drawn back in a neat bun, and she looked smart and efficient.

"How do you do?" she said, extending her hand. "I'm Ruthann Miller. I've applied to be your new sales manager. Let me explain some of my ideas for the company." Oh, she was sure of herself.

Russell Wayne Timmons, quieted, leaned back in his black leather chair. He swiveled in it while he watched the job applicant and listened. Pretty sharp. A tough cookie. Yes, you could always tell.

"And I suggest that some people be brought in from the outside. Workers with a variety of skills. I remember, from my high school days when I ran the Y.E.S. office, just how many people it takes to have a good service. No point in being understaffed, know what I mean?"

"Yes, Miss Miller, I do. Funny thing, your mentioning a Y.E.S. service. My older sister managed one when she was in school, so I see your point. When can you start work for the Timmons Company?"

FWEEEP! FWEEEEEEEP!
Rusty, jolted awake, sat up so abruptly that he clonked his head on the top bunk.

"Time to get up, Russell Wayne," Mike chirruped.

He put a hand to the throbbing place on his

head, where a bump was busy growing. Maybe it was time to separate the bunks. Maybe Mike would help him and he could drop a bunk on her. "Get out of my room! And take that whistle!" he added, needlessly.

"Motherrrr!" Mike's sandals clattered down the hall. "Rusty's being mean to me again!"

He lay back down. What a weird dream. Ruth-ann in a blue business suit. With her hair all fixed up. She'd looked really different, but nice. For once she hadn't called him Ketchup, either. And what a heck of an idea.

He sat back up, carefully this time. Yeah! What an idea! Three hundred dollars was practically in his pocket. Already he could picture Dan making a perfect lay-up on the new basketball court. And Rusty was there, ready to grab the rebound.

Rusty bounced to school, humming and mentally counting the pots of money that would come in from his new job service. He could call it Timmons' Total Service. The kids would love it because there was never anything to do in Hampshire during the summer and everyone died of boredom. But this summer they'd be busy earning money. He wondered if he should call

Mr. Tucker at the bike shop and tell him to stock up on new bikes. Some of Rusty's workers, for sure, would want to buy new bikes at the end of summer. Racing bikes with ten speeds, dirt bikes, BMXs—he could see them blooming all over town like mobile flowers.

"Hey, Ketchup! Wait up!"

Rusty stiffened as he heard Ruthann's flying footsteps. She often dashed up from behind and walked with him the last few blocks to school. Although they'd been in classes together since kindergarten, he didn't think of her as a close friend. She usually made him laugh, but she was too different. Too prickly. He couldn't imagine why he had dreamed about her.

"You're sure quiet. Worried about the math test?"

Rusty gave her his biggest smile. "Nope. Working on a great idea, that's all."

"Tell me about it." Ruthann tossed her sand-colored hair off her face and fixed him with a blue-eyed stare.

He looked away from the blueness of those eyes and debated about telling her his idea. Why not? He was going to tell the class all about it in a few hours at Debbie's party. No wonder she chose a blue suit, he thought. Matches her eyes. "Geez!" he said aloud. He must be cracking up.

"Tell me! What's bugging you?"

He pulled himself together. "I have had," he began grandly, "an awesome idea for summer. I'm going to tell everybody tonight at the party. You going to Debbie's house?"

"Depends."

"Depends on what?"

"On how I feel at the time. Most of our parties are pretty dumb." Ruthann jerked open the door of the school and strode in ahead of him. "See you in math."

"Tonight's party will be terrific," he called after her. "You'll be more interested than some of the kids," he added loudly, reasoning that anyone as poor as Ruthann would need to earn money.

The next-to-last day in school went on and on, the way it always does, but Rusty survived the math final and felt hopeful about his grade. He liked math almost as much as he liked science.

"A day *early,*" Rusty said to Mr. Ingram that afternoon as he placed his dolphin report on the teacher's desk.

"I see," nodded Mr. Ingram. "And what are you

going to do in class while everyone else copies reports?"

"I have work, don't worry. I'll be a mouse in the corner." Rusty grinned at him.

The teacher chuckled. "That'll be the day."

But Rusty sat quietly in class as he worked out his plan for Timmons' Total Service. He made a list of possible jobs and designed a poster to advertise the Service. Next, he wrote an ad that his mother could put in the newspaper. He knew the ad would cost money, but as manager he would have to pay business costs.

As pens scribbled busily around him, Rusty leaned back in his seat, content and confident. He wondered what percentage of their earnings the kids would be willing to give him as commission. If he asked too much, no one would want to work for him. If he asked too little, the Service wasn't worth the trouble. Finally, he fixed on ten percent. One thin dime out of everybody's dollar. Nobody's going to miss a measly dime, he decided. And of course Rusty would take some of the jobs himself. His dad, who managed a business in downtown Hampshire, had always told Rusty that workers need to see how hard the manager works.

School out, Rusty reassured Debbie about Julia's brownies and told her he was also bringing a surprise to her party.

"Great! Whisper it to me," Debbie said eagerly, sticking her ear right in his face.

"If I tell you," he said, backing away from her ear, "then it won't be a surprise." Rusty shut his locker door. "See you at seven-thirty."

Promptly at seven-thirty, brownies in hand, sign-up sheets folded in his pocket, Rusty rang the doorbell at Debbie Purdy's house. Half the class was already in the kitchen—pouring Cokes, ripping open bags of potato chips and putting cookies onto serving plates. Debbie's father was popping corn in a blackened pan, which he rattled back and forth over the gas burner on the stove.

The party grew in number and volume until eight o'clock, when Rusty judged that everyone who was coming was there. Even Ruthann had come, although she was sitting by herself in front of the TV set. She and Tiffany were the only ones not talking.

"When're you going to tell us your fantastic idea?" Dan asked Rusty. "Debbie told everyone you had a surprise, so we're all waiting."

"You're going to love it," promised Rusty, praying that Dan would become involved so that they could be together even before he got the basketball court. "Hey, everybody!" Rusty hollered. "It's terrific-idea time."

Gradually, conversations stopped as Debbie turned off the record player and groups of kids moved into position so that they could see Rusty.

"Get up on a chair, Ketchup!" Ruthann called from the far end of the family room. "All's I can see is your hair!"

Glowing pinkly, Rusty hopped onto a kitchen chair as kids giggled at her remark. Not for the first time he wished that somebody would stuff a sock in Ruthann Miller's mouth.

"Okay," he began, suddenly hesitant. Why had he been sure everyone would like his idea? "Okay," he repeated more firmly. "I am not going to be bored this summer like every other summer. What's more, I'm going to earn piles of money. Anybody interested in joining me?"

Cheers and whistles split the air. It was some time before he quieted them down and could begin speaking again. "I've started a service business, just like the Y.E.S. office in the high school, and anybody who wants can sign up with me for summer jobs. Most of them will be part-time, but that's okay, because we're not old enough to have full-time jobs anyway, and who wants to work every minute all summer?"

"Yeah, yeah!" Bob Matthews said. "I can mow lawns. Got my own tractor." He cleared his throat. "Well, Dad's tractor. But he won't care."

Rusty pointed a finger at Bob. *"He's* got the idea. I'll advertise our services in the newspaper and put up posters all over town. I'll take all the phone calls so your folks won't be bothered. A real service, like my business, can get lots more jobs than any of us working alone. I know, because I've been trying to earn money for over a month and all I've got is twenty-three dollars after today's job."

"What do you get out of it?" Ruthann asked. "Sounds like a giant pain. All those phone calls, *ack!"*

"My folks won't care," he said bravely. He hadn't discussed his idea with his parents yet, but surely they would see what a good plan it was.

"I take the phone calls," he continued, "because that's a manager's job. I pay for newspaper ads and posters and stuff, because those are the costs of running a business. For that I get a commission—just ten percent. For every dollar I get you in a job, you give me one dime. That's all."

His classmates shuffled their feet and turned to talk to nearby friends. Rusty waited and felt extremely self-conscious up on his chair. This was the crucial moment. If they didn't trust the idea to work, or didn't trust him to make it work, then Timmons' Total Service was doomed.

"Rusty? I've got an idea!" Priscilla Boden waved her hand in the air and smiled at him. She smoothed a too-tight T-shirt down over her hips. Bob watched and emitted a loud wolf whistle.

"Oh brother," Ruthann moaned. "Any idea *she'll* have is illegal."

Priscilla shot a withering look in Ruthann's direction, then turned to Rusty. "Listen, I have a terrific idea. Me and Dawn want to run a Meals-On-Wheels-type business like they talk about on radio, you know? We can make lunches and suppers for people who are old or sick and shut in."

"Yeah!" Dawn Wetherington, a tall girl who was usually quiet, waved her hand in the air.

"We're good cooks, really we are. Doesn't that sound like *fun*?"

Rusty blinked in surprise. He had never even considered cooking as a possible job. "Isn't that an awful lot of work?" he asked Dawn and Priscilla.

"Don't blow yourself out of the water, Ketchup." No longer sitting, Ruthann was standing up, hands on hips. And again, the two adjoining rooms of kids laughed at Rusty.

"Thank you, thank you," Rusty said, trying to sound pleasant instead of annoyed.

"You're welcome." Ruthann made a mock bow. "You're all missing the point—except for Dawnsy and Prissy. Since the Y.E.S. service is closed, *we'll* get those part-time jobs, or most of them, because the older kids take full-time summer jobs. And we can work in pairs or groups, which's a lot more fun than working alone. Two can mow and trim a lawn in half the time and do twice as many a day, see? The people who hire us'll be impressed at how fast we work. Parents may pay more for sitters who come in pairs because their kids will get better care." Ruthann tossed her hair back in a swift motion and sat down where Rusty couldn't see her.

Before anyone could speak, she shot upward again. "And we'd be smart to sign up kids from other grades, too. The more services we can offer, the better we'll look and the more business we'll get." She frowned in concentration. "I guess that's it. Anyway, *I'm* signing up because summer's so boring I could just croak."

Rusty closed his mouth, which had fallen open fishlike during her speech. "I did bring some sign-up sheets, in case anybody was interested." He pulled them from his back pocket. "Just write your name and phone number, and a list of jobs you're interested in."

"Give me one," Bob Matthews said, reaching forward.

"Us, too," chimed Dawn and Priscilla.

"I'll think about it," Dan said, extending his hand. "It sure is a heck of an idea."

"Dan, don't you think we're going to be awfully busy?" Tiffany's voice was low. "Champagne's brother comes this weekend, so we'll have two horses to exercise. And his stall isn't finished."

Dan withdrew the hand that had been held out to Rusty. "Well, look, I'll think about it. Dad said I ought to be earning my own spending money."

"Sure, Dan." Rusty gave the sign-up sheet to

another hand stretched above the crowd. "Sign up anytime you want."

Before the end of the party, Rusty had given away all the sheets he had prepared. Twenty kids had been ready to work for Timmons' Total Service, and several more were planning to make their own sign-up sheets and give them to Rusty in school the next day.

At nine-thirty Rusty thanked Debbie and let himself out the Purdys' front door. As he stepped onto the porch, he heard the creak of the Purdys' ancient swing. "Thought I'd walk home with you. In case you're afraid of the dark." Ruthann's mocking voice was unmistakable.

He couldn't be mad at her this time. She had "clinched the deal," as his dad would say, overcoming any doubts their classmates might have had about Rusty's idea. "Thanks," he said as she fell into step beside him. "You made it easy."

"Don't thank *me*! I need your job service to work. If I don't put myself through college, nobody else will, that's for sure. Even Ohio State costs a fortune, and I'm not sure they have what I want."

Rusty was impressed. "How do you know what you want to do?"

"I *always* know. I'm going to major in genet-
ics."

"Genes and things?"

"You got it. I want to find out what makes people the way they are, what things can be inher-
ited and what can't and why. All that stuff about
environment is crap."

In the dark, Rusty grinned. The image of
Ruthann in the navy-blue suit was clear in his
mind.

"Here's my street. When do we start work?"

"Well, let's see. I have to put an ad in the paper—"

"Put the posters up first," she interrupted.
"They'll work right away. Paper doesn't come
out till next Wednesday."

"Okay, okay," he answered easily. She sure
was pushy.

"I'll come over to your place Saturday morning," Ruthann announced. "That way I can help
make posters. I've got more good ideas, too.
Night." She vanished in the dark around her
house, leaving Rusty on the sidewalk.

3

One More Manager

Friday evening the phone rang in the Timmons kitchen and Rusty picked up the receiver. "Commence," he said solemnly, his mouth twitching at the corners.

"Uh, is this Rusty's house?"

"Dan?"

"Yeah. Is that you?"

"Sure. How's things?"

"Okay, but I had to tell you I won't be working with you just yet."

Rusty gripped the phone, his vacation good humor oozing away.

"See, Champagne's brother is coming this weekend. He's a palomino too, only darker, Tiffany said. We think we're going to name him Brandy—isn't that cool?"

"Yeah, cool. Remember the summer our camp dog Susie had her puppies and we named one Brandy because he was sort of a goldy-brown?"

"Right. Don't tell Tiffany, though. She thinks I've got a great imagination. I'd almost forgotten Susie. That whole camp was out of sight. I couldn't believe all the boats we had. And remember that old canvas canoe we took over the rocks and just shredded!" Dan cackled gleefully at the memory.

"I'm surprised they asked us back after that one. I'd kind of like to go back, too—be in the oldest cabin, you know? But it's time I was earning money. That's why I started the job service."

"Dad's itchy for me to get a job. But I can probably put it off for a few more weeks. I'll let you know as soon as I can. Maybe lawns or something like that."

"Just let me know. I'd hate to have all the good jobs taken by somebody else."

"Sure. Well, I'm going to Tiffany's to watch a movie. See you around."

Rusty hung up. No, he thought, you probably won't see me around. Not if you're at Tiffany's all the time.

"Rusty, I didn't mean to eavesdrop," Mrs. Timmons said, "but what was that about jobs being 'taken by somebody else'?" She pushed her glasses up into her hair and blinked at him.

"I have had the most awesome idea," Rusty said carefully, wanting to get the conversation off to a good start.

"I'll bet. Does Dad know about your awesome idea?"

"I don't think so, but he's going to love it."

"Wayne?" called Mrs. Timmons. "Can you come into the kitchen for a few minutes?" She sat down at the table and began tapping a pencil. "I hope I am going to love it," she said apprehensively.

"Dad," Rusty said as soon as his father appeared, "I need your advice about how to run my business. See, I started a business . . ."

The pencil tapping increased.

"Mom, don't get excited. I'm going to be busy with work all summer, so while you're at the office and Dad's at his office, nobody will have to worry about me. Julia won't have to baby-sit for me, just Mike, and that ought to be a snap."

"What kind of business is it?" his father asked.

Rusty explained his idea of a kids' job service, being sure to mention the enthusiasm of his newly recruited workers.

When he finished, his dad nodded. "Sounds

good to me. You ought to be able to pick up right where the Y.E.S. office left off. But are you sure your workers will report all their earnings? And what if they get their own jobs?"

"I expect them to be honest! I mean, I'm going to all the work of setting it up."

Mr. Timmons smiled knowingly. "Just think about it, that's all."

"They won't all be here at the house, will they?" his mother asked. "You know I write at home sometimes, and Wednesday, after the paper is out, I sit by my pool. *In peace.*"

"Anne, Rusty won't have the workers here, and we all know how much that pool means to you. Right, Russ?"

Rusty knew. His mother had saved her salary for two years to pay for the large aboveground pool that sat at the rear of the Timmons backyard. It was her prize possession. "No sweat, Mom. I promise." He made several more promises—about asking his parents' advice whenever he had to make a difficult decision and about not hogging the telephone.

Mr. Timmons rose from the table. "I think it sounds like an exciting summer. Just be sure," he said as he headed back to the television, "that you don't take any dangerous jobs. We wouldn't want to be sued."

"Lord," moaned Mrs. Timmons, who never swore.

"See what I mean?" Mr. Timmons shook his finger at Rusty. "This is serious business, and you have to run it that way."

Gravely, Rusty promised. Inside, though, he wanted to shout *yahoo!* Now it was official. He was in business for himself.

"I just wish I didn't have these awful premonitions," Mrs. Timmons said, standing up. "I keep thinking—"

"Don't think, Mom," Rusty soothed, as he had many times in the past. She, unlike Rusty, was a natural worrier. "Just go on back to your article and don't give it another thought."

His mother smiled vaguely. "I wish I could operate the way you do," she said as she went back to work in the den.

FWEEP! FWEEEEEP! The whistle shrilled right through Rusty's bedroom door. Rusty pulled his pillow over his head.

"Michelle!" Mr. Timmons' voice, low but penetrating, came through the door as well. "Scoot! You'll wake your mother, and she was up late working. Rusty?" The voice grew louder as his dad opened the door and poked his head into the room. "The Miller girl—Ruthann is it?—well, she's downstairs. She said you had an appointment to work on posters." He chuckled. "Doesn't know you like to sleep late, does she?" The door shut and Rusty rolled over to peer groggily at his watch. Seven-thirty.

"Seven-thirty?" he groaned in shock. It was the middle of the night! Ruthann was crazy. What's more, she had invited herself. He had never really told anyone off, but now he was going to. Who did she think she was, anyhow?

Rusty pulled on jeans and an old soccer T-shirt and stumbled downstairs barefoot, hair rumpled, eyes half shut.

"Hi there, Bubbles," Ruthann drawled as he lurched into the kitchen.

"Mmmmfff," Rusty mumbled, gathering his anger as he peered at her across the room.

Ruthann giggled. "God, you look like the morning after."

His head jerked up. "Don't swear. My folks don't allow it."

"Oh. Your dad a preacher or something?"

"He teaches Sunday school. At Hampshire First Presbyterian."

"My mom says she's outgrown church. Gramma goes sometimes, but I don't. Let's get to work. Then we can put up posters this afternoon."

Rusty shook his head. He wondered what Reverend Parker would say about outgrowing church. And there she was again, managing *his* business. Ordering him around. "Look, Ruthann," he said grimly.

"Peace!" She held up one hand and waved it like a white flag. "I see I woke you up. But I was so hot to get started that I bought some Magic Markers yesterday. And I've got a terrific idea for a poster, with a slogan and everything."

"It is the first morn-ing of va-ca-tion," Rusty began.

Impatiently, Ruthann nodded.

"And I love to *sleep late*—"

"You can't run a business from bed!" She slammed the packet of Magic Markers down on the table.

"Who do you think you are?" Rusty glared at her. He loathed arguments, and here he was, leaping right into one.

Ruthann straightened. "I'm the only one who volunteered to help, that's who! I paid for these Magic Markers myself, instead of saving the money for a blouse, which I *need*. I made a whole bunch of new sign-up sheets to pass out whenever I see somebody who'd work for you. *Everybody else is home in bed.*"

Defeated, Rusty pulled out a chair and sat down at the kitchen table. He ran both hands through his hair, making all of it stand up in jagged spikes, like a rooster with several red combs instead of one.

Again she giggled, but more softly. "*Please,*" she said, "just look at my poster. It's short, so it won't take long to make, and it's *memorable.* That's the best part. People'll remember it." She darted into the front hall and came back unrolling the poster. She opened it to its full length and stood back, waiting.

TIMMONS' TOTAL SERVICE

Job Need Doing?
Give US a call.
Our TOTAL SERVICE
Does them ALL!

Phone:
Rusty Timmons, Manager
555-6207
or Ruthann miller, 555-8918

TIMMONS' TOTAL SERVICE

When he had read as far as her name and number, Rusty gasped.

"Don't say anything! Just listen to me." She rolled up the poster and held it against her chest.

Rusty stared at her. She needn't have worried about his speaking. He couldn't imagine what to say.

"I have to earn a ton of money. You know why. And I can help a whole lot. I'll make the posters, I'll put 'em up, I'll take phone calls. See, at my house it won't matter. Nobody ever calls us anyway, so nobody cares how much I'm on the phone. I know the girls and what they can do, and you don't. There's good money in something like Prissy's meal service idea. And I'll take the jobs that nobody else wants. *I can do anything.*"

Rusty was fully awake now. "Okay, okay. Just *relax,* okay?"

Clutching the poster, Ruthann waited.

"This is *my* business. If we're going to argue all the time, then you can't help."

"I won't argue."

"You will too!"

"I WILL NOT!" flared Ruthann. Then, more softly, "I'll try not to, really I will. It's your business. I'd just like first crack at some of the jobs, and maybe I can earn that by working for the Service."

Rusty thought for several seconds, and the only sound in the kitchen was the ticking clock. "I guess that's fair." He paused. "And that's a great poster. Better than mine."

Ruthann was silent.

"You won't make any of the workers mad? You won't call them names? This's a business, remember?"

Ruthann opened her mouth, then shut it. "Right," she said finally.

"Can I have breakfast now?"

She shrugged. "Why not? I'll start on the posters."

"You want something?"

"I never eat breakfast." Ruthann began laying out the Magic Markers, admiring their clean new points, touching each one respectfully.

As he poured milk on his cereal, Rusty watched her. She was thin almost to the point of being bony. What if they didn't have enough to eat at her house? He crunched his cereal slowly, thinking how he would hate to miss breakfast. When he made toast, he fixed two pieces, spreading them liberally with honey. "Here," he said, handing her one on a plate. "I'm too full to eat this one. Don't know why I made it."

Ruthann accepted the toast. She took small bites, making it last a long time. "You know," she said, licking honey from her forefinger, "we're going to make a fortune this summer."

"A million at least," he agreed, feeling better. "I'll get the paper I bought for posters. You don't have much there. And I ought to pay for the markers. That's a business expense."

"No," she said. "If I paid for them, I can keep them when we're done."

"Okay." As he went to get the poster paper he wondered if the whole summer would be like this short, painful morning. How could he have let her talk him into so much? And what would she want next?

Unsmiling, he sat down at the table and began to copy the poster. It took him twice as long as Ruthann to do each one, and his were not as professional looking. He held up his third poster, eyeing it critically. "Mine are terrible."

"They're okay, but mine are better. I love making posters. Why don't you make a list of prices for jobs? I don't know much about that. Make our prices a little lower than you think kids've been

charging. That way we'll beat out any competition."

A chuckle rumbled in the kitchen doorway, and Rusty looked up to see his dad grinning at Ruthann. "You have business bones, girl. You might have the workers mention your low prices to their customers, too, if you want, and say that they'll accept tips if the employers are happy with the work. The kids could keep any tips, of course. They'd like that, wouldn't they?"

"Great idea, Mr. T. Why don't you help Rusty with the job prices? That is, if you're not busy."

"All right," agreed Rusty's dad, joining them at the table.

Later, Mrs. Timmons, Julia and Mike took their breakfast to the wicker table on the back porch so that work could go on undisturbed.

When the price list was finished, Mr. Timmons said, "Looks good. Nice, competitive prices. Are you sure the kids will agree to work for these hourly rates?"

"No, we're not," Ruthann answered before Rusty could speak.

"Yes we are," he insisted, frowning at her. "I'll call them and explain the rates and Dad's idea for earning tips. They'll be fine if I tell them it's going to bring us more business."

"If *you* explain it, they'll probably agree." Ruthann flexed the fingers of her right hand. "I don't love making posters as much as I did a few hours ago, but they're all done."

"That's amazing," Mr. Timmons said, smiling at Ruthann over the tall stack of completed signs.

"She started at dawn." Rusty yawned and stretched.

"It's a good thing. Now we can put them up all over town and make a worker list to hang by our telephones. Come on." She stood up.

"How about lunch?" Rusty suggested.

"Look, Chubsie, we just finished breakfast!"

"It's noon! Can't you hear the noon whistle in town? And I haven't cleaned up. I can't go downtown yet."

"*I'll* start putting up posters." Ruthann grabbed the pile off the table.

"Believe I'll go work in the yard." Mr. Timmons rose from his seat and headed for the back door. He looked over his shoulder and winked at Rusty as he went out the door.

"This isn't going to work if you don't slow down," Rusty told Ruthann when his dad was out of earshot.

"Well you can't just eat and sleep!"

"You said you weren't going to argue!" Rusty felt his face growing pinker. Of course she would argue. She was going to argue all summer.

Rusty looked down at his bare feet and said nothing. Ruthann looked at the wall. Both of them listened to the ticking clock.

Finally she took a step toward him. "Look, Rusty, I'll get a big Band-Aid to tape over my mouth. I'll look weird, but at least I'll be quiet. Got any Band-Aids?"

"They're upstairs. I'll bring one down after I've cleaned up." Rusty marched past her and stomped up the steps to his room.

4

The Power of Advertising

As he pounded the last thumbtack into a poster, Rusty was his old self. Ruthann hadn't said a word for twenty posters. She couldn't. The largest Timmons Band-Aid was stretched tightly across her mouth.

"Job need do-oo-ing, give us a call," Rusty sang softly as he debated where to put another poster. It was one o'clock, and the First Presbyterian's carillon tower was playing "Amazing Grace," a tune that was perfect for the Timmons' Total Service slogan. "Our to-ta-al ser-vice does them all," he caroled happily.

"Unh, unh," Ruthann grunted, pointing to a telephone pole on her right. She hadn't seemed to mind the stares the Band-Aid had earned her from townspeople. She was all business.

A car stopped by the curb near the telephone pole and Mrs. Timmons leaned out the window. "I'll be at the office for a few hours. We've got a problem." She eyed Ruthann, who was thumb-tacking the poster. "Rusty, why does she have a Band-Aid over her mouth?"

"Guess," he said, grinning.

"I don't have time. Just tell me."

"She was arguing too much. It was her idea!"

Rusty's mother rubbed a hand over her fore-head. "I think you should encourage her to take it off. And your posters look wonderful, by the way. I never knew anybody could wallpaper an entire town. I've got your ad for the service in my purse. If you want it to run for three weeks, it'll cost nine dollars."

Above the Band-Aid, Ruthann's eyes grew wide.

That would leave only ten dollars in Rusty's blue safe, because poster paper had cost four dollars. Thirteen dollars in expenses and he hadn't even started business. "I guess we have to do it," he said slowly.

Ruthann nodded vigorously.

"Take the Band-Aid off, dear," Mrs. Timmons urged her.

R-r-r-iiip! "Of course we have to do it! You have to spend money to make money!" She turned to Mrs. Timmons. "I read that somewhere, and I just know it's true."

"It makes sense, doesn't it? I have to go now, but say hello to your gramma for me, won't you? When I was a girl and she was our town librarian, I remember thinking that she'd read every book in our library." Rusty's mother smiled at the memory, waved and drove away.

"Gramma reads all the time," Ruthann said proudly, her small, pointed chin jutting forward. "She's always telling me to turn off the TV, but I do what I want."

"Let's finish these posters," Rusty said, changing the subject. "Did you read the workers' sign-up sheets while I was changing clothes?"

"Yup. Annie Emline signed up to pool-sit." Ruthann snorted. "Who wouldn't?"

"There are real good ones, though. About four or five yard workers, lots of baby-sitters and housecleaners, the meal-service thing and Fred Jenkins has this giant cat who's a mouser. He's going to call his business Jenkins' Rent-A-Cat."

"Fancy Fred?" Ruthann asked, referring to Fred's preference for dressier clothes than most of the kids typically wore.

"Ruthann!"

Her hand flew to her mouth. Posters number twenty-two and twenty-three were put into place in total silence.

As Ruthann taped a poster to a downtown florist's window, she spoke up again. "I had a great idea for Mabel Ann McSpurgeon."

"But she's a sophomore. Did she sign up?"

"No, but she's going to. She's crazy about little kids, so I'm going to suggest she run a summer play school as part of the Service business. We can tell everyone who calls that she's doing it, and it ought to be worth a fortune."

"Yeah!" he agreed readily. I never would have thought of that, he said to himself. "How about putting a poster across the street, on Old Doc's window?" Without waiting for her answer, he zipped over to the vet's office, reappearing a minute later to wave her across the street.

"Right in this corner," he told her, pointing to the place Old Doc had suggested.

That one taped in place, the two surveyed the street. Nearly every building and telephone pole bore a new Timmons poster.

"Hi. What're you doing?" A slender boy carrying a dark-gray cat came out the door of the vet's office.

"Hi, Marty." Ruthann reached in the back pocket of her jeans. "Why don't you sign up to work with pets? See?" She gestured at the window and offered him a sign-up sheet at the same time.

"Yeah, I meant to do that," Marty said as he read the poster.

"I'll hold the cat while you fill out the paper," Ruthann said, lifting Eleanor out of Marty's arms.

"All pet care, okay?" he told Rusty as he gave him the sign-up sheet. "Clipping parakeets' toenails, grooming and bathing, walking dogs, everything. And thanks a lot." He smiled at both of them, picked Eleanor out of Ruthann's arms and waved good-bye. "Thanks, Ruthann," he said again as he rounded the corner.

Dazed, Rusty said to Ruthann, "You did that great."

Ruthann scowled. "I can be nice when I have to. Come on, let's go to your place and make the list of workers. Then when somebody calls, we'll know who does what. We'll have to keep another list that says when people already have jobs so we don't send somebody to two places at once."

"No," he said, bracing himself.

"Why not?"

"It's after two and I still haven't had lunch. And besides, I feel like . . . like a yo-yo!"

"Are you saying I'm bossy again?"

Rusty nodded, his mouth set in a firm line.

After a bit, Ruthann unexpectedly smiled. "Okay. When, *Mister Timmons*, would you like me to come over to do the list of workers?"

He didn't want her to come at all, but he couldn't bring himself to say that. "Oh, later this afternoon, I guess."

"But *when*?"

"Around four?" Why couldn't she relax?

"I'll be there. Maybe then I'll know about Mabel Ann. I'll go see her now. 'Bye!" She whirled and took off down the street, pale hair swinging behind her, and Rusty walked toward home.

After lunch, Rusty looked for Julia. She had a date with Greg that night, so he figured she'd be in her room getting gorgeous.

"Julia?" he called outside her bedroom door.

"I'm doing my nails. What do you want?"

"Just to talk. Can I come in?"

Once inside the room, Rusty sprawled on Julia's bed, pillowing his head on her old Pooh bear. He gazed at the ceiling, wondering how to begin.

Julia held one hand out to admire the polish. "Well, what is it? Dad said you made a ton of posters this morning."

"*She* did. They're up already. All over town. And Mom said she'd put my ad in the paper."

"So what's the problem?" Julia blew on her nails to dry the polish.

"Ruthann. She's doing everything." Rusty sat up on the bed. "She's taking over!"

"Oh come on, Rusty."

"I'm not kidding!" He told his sister all that had happened since Debbie's party. "And she's coming over in just a little while so we can make worker lists. I would have done it, but I don't see what the rush is."

"You're the manager, not her. Just get tough."

"But I can't go around saying, *'I'm the manager, I'm the manager!'* all the time," Rusty shouted, waving his hands in the air. He caught sight of himself in Julia's mirror and had to laugh. He looked ridiculous.

Julia laughed with him. "Look, Rusty, give her a break. You do things *your* way, and she does things *her* way, but after a while you'll rub off on her, know what I mean? She's had it rough, you know that. Maybe this is the first time she's been involved in something with kids. I'll bet she'll learn if you give her a chance."

The telephone rang before Rusty could tell Julia that she was being wildly optimistic.

"I'll get that," Julia said, leaping off her chair. "It's probably for me." But it wasn't. "Phone's for you," she told him, coming back into the room. "Don't be long, because Greg's supposed to call any minute."

Rusty went into his parents' room, where the upstairs phone was located. "Hello."

"Is this Timmons' Service? I'd like to speak to Rusty Timmons."

"Sure! I mean, yes, this is Timmons' Total Service. What can we do for you?" His voice shook with excitement. Rusty listened to the voice on the other end of the phone. "I'll just run downstairs to the other phone where our workers are listed, Mrs. Benton. Please hold on."

Rusty pelted downstairs and flipped madly through the sign-up sheets. "Hello? I'd like to recommend Molly Lemon and Lynn Gail Cleary. If you've got five kids, you'd probably be a lot happier with two sitters, and they work as a pair. Can I give you their phone numbers?"

Seconds later, Rusty hung up the phone and shouted, "YAHOOO!"

FWEEEP! FWEEEP! Mike appeared at Rusty's elbow. "No shouting! Dad's takin' a nap."

"Not anymore I'm not." Mr. Timmons' voice clearly reached the kitchen from the adjoining family room. "Was that a job for your service?"

"Yeah! Two baby-sitters. For a new family in town."

A brief knock sounded at the back screen door, and then Ruthann was in the kitchen. "Did I hear right? Did somebody call already?"

Rusty explained the call. "And she saw our poster at the supermarket. She said it was a great poster and just when she needed it."

"Well," Ruthann said quietly, as if she could hardly believe the news.

The phone rang again. "Timmons' Total Service," Rusty warbled. Ruthann leaned forward.

"Of course we can." Rusty listened and nodded. "Where did you see our poster?" Then, "You didn't? Yes, I walk Mrs. Wayland's dogs." Silence. "Yes, we can have someone there tomorrow. . . . Five dollars *a day*?" His voice rose in amazement. "You're welcome, sir. And thank you for calling."

Ruthann wrapped her arms around her body as if to contain herself. "Five bucks a day? What for?"

"For one hour's work! Just one hour exercising an old pony! It's a man named Langendorfer. He lives next to Waylands', and he got my name from them."

"Then he wants you."

"I don't know anything about horses. Who signed up for that?"

"Nobody," Ruthann said flatly. "And Marty Howard works with house pets. Are you sure you don't want to do it?"

Rusty hesitated. "Well, it's an *old* pony. He belonged to Mr. Langendorfer's brother who had him in the circus. Now the brother's dead and Mr. Langendorfer's got the pony, but it doesn't sound like a nice pony. We should send somebody who knows horses."

"I'll do it," she said, almost before he'd finished speaking.

"You know horses?" Rusty asked doubtfully.

"What's there to know? I can read, can't I? A pony's a pony." Her confidence was overwhelming.

Rusty thought about what Mr. Langendorfer had said about the pony. "But this one—" he began worriedly.

"Now *you're* the one who's arguing!" Her blue eyes bored into him. "Just tell me where to go and when. Every hour I work that pony's worth four-fifty to me and fifty cents to you. Think of it that way."

Rusty shrugged. "Okay," he said as the phone rang again.

"That better be for me!" Julia called as her feet pounded down the steps. She tore into the kitchen and grabbed the phone off the hook. "Oh, hi, Greg," she said breathlessly. "I'll bet you had trouble getting through. My brother's been on the phone *all day*."

Rusty rolled his eyes heavenward. He motioned to Ruthann, and they sat down at the kitchen table, workers' sign-up sheets in front of them. They began by listing the various jobs that were possible, with workers' names ranked below the type of job. At one point Rusty looked up at the clock. Almost five, and Julia was still talking to Greg. She had pulled the long cord out of the kitchen and was huddled in a corner of the dining room.

"Hey, Julia. That phone's my business, you know!"

Julia put a hand over the receiver. "And since when have you been paying the phone bill around here?"

"Come on, *please.* You've been on almost an hour! Probably cost me a fortune already."

"Greg? Look, I've got to go. I'll be ready at seven-thirty." Julia and the phone receiver returned to the kitchen. "I hope you're happy, Rusty. I'm going to talk to Dad about this. You can't monopolize the phone *all summer*." Her shoes slapped the linoleum as she stalked out of the kitchen.

"I knew it," Ruthann said smugly. "We can start telling people to call my house, and that way they'll call here only the first time."

Rusty leaned his chair back on two legs. Well, maybe it wasn't so awful that her name was on the poster—and her phone number. The phone calls hadn't seemed like any big deal, but it looked as if they would be. "Let's quit for now," he suggested. "We're all organized, and it's hot in here. We could get in the pool, okay?"

Ruthann started to say something, then clamped her lips shut. She stood up and pushed her chair into the table. "I can start exercising that pony in the morning, right?"

"That's what he said, but—"

"Then I better go home and read about horses."

"Don't you want to swim?"

"I drown easy. See you in the morning."

"After church. If anybody calls on Sunday mornings, I hope they call you."

"They will. They have both numbers from the poster. See ya." She left before Rusty could say anything more. He wasn't sure what he would have said anyway. She was the strangest girl.

5

A Booming Business

At breakfast Sunday morning, Mr. Timmons informed Julia that she was to share the phone with Rusty and his business.

"I need my own phone," Julia muttered.

"You can't watch Michelle and talk on the phone," Mrs. Timmons said. "That's a paying job, remember?"

"It'll only be busy at first!" Rusty protested. "After people have workers it'll slow down. And we're telling all the callers to use Ruthann's number whenever they can." He didn't want to fight with Julia. Ruthann was enough to deal with.

"We'll see." Julia's skepticism was obvious.

*

Later, Mr. Timmons patted Rusty's shoulder on his way through the kitchen. "Family's in the car, Russ."

Rusty, phone in hand, nodded. "Gotta go, Ruthann. We'll be in church till twelve, like I said."

"Better you than me. Talk to you later. I already exercised that dumb pony. 'Bye."

Rusty charged out the door. Ruthann didn't seem to like the pony any better than Mr. Langendorfer did. Still, it was five dollars a day. The idea that he'd already made fifty cents from the pony job filled his mind with glee. This service business had to be the best idea anybody'd ever had.

After church, the Timmons family were on their way to the car when a boy approached them. "Here is my sign-up sheet, Rusty. I'm sorry to be late, but I only got it from Ruthann yesterday." One hand held out a folded piece of paper. His other hand strayed toward his face and began stroking his nose.

Rusty froze in place.

"Hello, Jeremy," Mrs. Timmons said. "How are your parents?"

"They are both home today. My father is recuperating from a heart attack again. It's only a small one this time, but my mother is afraid to leave him," Jeremy said in his odd, formal way. One finger continued to stroke his nose. "Here, Rusty," he repeated, urging the folded paper forward.

Rusty felt everyone looking at him. He had no choice. He took the paper in two fingers and shoved it quickly into his pocket.

"What do you say, Russ?" His father looked at him sternly.

"Uh, thanks, Jermy. *Jeremy*. I'll . . . I'll call you soon as we get anything." Rusty nodded stiffly in Jeremy's direction, then walked to the car, opened the door and got in. Jeremy walked off in the opposite direction.

When all of the family were in the car, Mrs. Timmons turned to look at Rusty in the backseat. "I don't understand you! The Johnsons are a lovely family! You acted as if Jeremy had leprosy."

"I shoulda blown my whistle," Mike inserted.

Julia shook her head at Mike and turned to smile sympathetically at Rusty. "Now that's going to be a tough one."

"We're waiting, Russ," Mr. Timmons said as

he started the car engine and pulled away from the curb.

"He picks his nose," Rusty said abruptly. "I told you about him in kindergarten, and every year he's worse. Picks his nose constantly. That's why we call him Jermy. Nobody touches *anything* he touches if they can help it."

Mike leaned around Julia to stare at Rusty, fascinated. Both Mr. and Mrs. Timmons were rigidly silent in the front seat.

"We had our share of weirdos in the Y.E.S. office," Julia volunteered in the silence. "We had to work with them."

Rusty said nothing.

"Poor Roberta Johnson," Mrs. Timmons said. "I wonder if she knows about Jeremy?"

"Poor Jeremy," replied Mr. Timmons. "That's a psychological problem from the sound of things, and that kid needs help."

Amen, Rusty thought. Instead, to change the subject, he said, "Mom, is the ad in a good place? I'll bet all our workers have jobs before the ad runs out."

Rusty had changed his clothes and was building a triple-decker peanut-butter-and-jelly when the Timmonses' phone rang. "Timmons' Total Service," he said as he spread the jelly.

"Oh, Rusty," pealed Priscilla's voice in his ear, "you don't have to sell *me!*" She giggled.

Rusty closed his eyes and took a bite of his sandwich. He had always worked at getting along with everyone in the class—not counting Jermy, of course—but Priscilla Boden was a flake. "What do you want?" he asked thickly through the peanut butter.

"You know we're running a meal service," she began.

"Yeah," he said encouragingly.

"Well, we've got a job! We're supposed to start tonight to see if this little old lady likes us. She wants supper every other night, 'cause she plays bingo, see?"

"Hey, that's great!"

"Yeah, well, my mom said you could only have ten percent of our meal profit, not the food cost. Each time, we'll have to deduct the food cost before we know what our profit is."

"That's fair. Did this lady see our posters?"

"In the ladies' john at church. I got two posters about our meal service from Ruthann, who made 'em special for me, and I put 'em up before church this morning." Priscilla took a breath and rushed on. "We set supper prices at four dollars and lunches at three dollars, if that's okay, and see, tonight we really wanted to make it special, since it's our first time and all."

"Rusty, I need the phone." Julia stood right next to him. She was still dressed for church and the toe of one high heel tap-tapped on the floor.

Rusty nodded okay at Julia while in his ear Priscilla carried on describing the Italian supper she and Dawn planned to fix. "And we've got this old red-checkered tablecloth and napkin—"

"I said I need the phone!" Tap, tap, tap.

FWEEEP! FWEEEEEP! "Want me to blow more, Julia?" Mike inhaled noisily and poised the whistle an inch from her mouth.

"Hang on, Priscilla." Rusty held the receiver against his stomach to block out sound. "Julia, this's our meal service and it's their first night. She's kind of excited and I'm trying to be helpful."

The high heel stopped tapping. Julia considered him a bit. "Okay, but I want it the minute you're done."

Rusty promised and waved Mike away. She stuck her tongue out at him but followed Julia

into the family room.

"Your meal sounds great. The prices are fair, too, but I have to hang up now, Priscilla."

"Wait, Rusty! I have to have some oregano!"

"Some what?"

"It's a spice. We need it for Italian spaghetti sauce."

"Ask Dawn, then."

"She's here! And *nobody's* got any oregano! I checked with Ruthann, and the store out on the highway is closed. Ask your mom if she's got some we could borrow."

Rusty went hunting for his mother, who said that the meal service was welcome to her oregano. "No more borrowing, Mom. It's just unlucky that Sunday's their first day and all the stores are closed. I don't think they were ready for this."

"I'm not sure *I* am," his mother said, but she smiled. "We'd planned for a quiet family day around the pool, you know. I hope you won't be involved all afternoon."

Rusty patted her red curls reassuringly, something he loved doing now that he was an inch taller than her modest five feet one. "Not to worry, little one," he said, grinning. On the phone, he told Priscilla to come get the oregano and hung up as quickly as he could. "It's all yours, Julia," he called out.

Just then Ruthann came in through the back screen door. Rusty took a big bite of his triple decker before he nodded hello.

"I talked Mabel Ann into the idea of a play school," Ruthann said. "Didn't take much talking. She's on the phone right now to some of the mothers she baby-sits for, and I told her we'd tell everyone who called about her school. She could have eight or ten, she thought. Mornings only. At"—she paused significantly—"*ten bucks a head. Every week.*"

"Wow! A hundred dollars a week!" He multiplied rapidly. "For eleven weeks. That's over a thousand dollars!"

Ruthann shook her head. "She won't have ten every week. Vacations and camp and stuff get in the way. But she could average maybe five or six a week. That's still good."

Rusty munched his sandwich. "That commission's yours," he said, swallowing. "I'd never have thought of it, and I'll bet Mabel Ann wouldn't either. Anyway, I hardly know her. She belongs to you."

"It's *your* business," Ruthann retorted, chin in

the air. "And I already got the pony job."

"That's right. It's *my* business. And *I* say Mabel Ann belongs to you. Now tell me about the pony, okay?"

"You're sure about that?" Ruthann asked, strangely polite. "I didn't think of it just so I could get the commission."

"I know. Don't sweat it. Tell me about the pony."

Ruthann held up a bandaged knee. "He's a real sweetie. Scraped me against his fence. But I'll outsmart him the next time. No stupid horse is going to run *me* around!"

Rusty frowned, thinking of what his dad had said about dangerous jobs. "Did you have to groom him afterward?" He had unpleasant visions of slender Ruthann dodging horse hooves in a dark stall.

Before she could reply, the phone rang again. Rusty referred the caller to Bob Matthews and his lawn tractor, then gave Ruthann's number for future Service calls. As he hung up, Priscilla Boden arrived to get the oregano. Ruthann entered Mabel Ann McSpurgeon's name on the worker chart and wrote "Play School" in every morning slot, five days a week. Bob called to say he'd be mowing and trimming the Rogiers' lawn every Friday morning with Fred Jenkins as a work partner. Ruthann marked the chart.

The Timmons family came and went in the kitchen, maneuvering around Rusty, Ruthann and the telephone cord. Fred Jenkins stopped by to say that his cat, Bismarck, had fur balls and wouldn't be available as Jenkins' Rent-A-Cat for a while, but he was sure glad about the mowing job with Bob.

Several friendly adults phoned to say they'd seen Rusty's signs and would call him if they needed workers. Rusty asked them to please call Ruthann in the future, and he told them about Mabel Ann's school. More people called to hire help, which Rusty happily assigned—two baby-sitters and three sets of housecleaning workers.

At five-thirty Ruthann said, "Guess I'll go home and see if my phone's ringing like this." And by seven, everyone in the family jumped when the phone rang. Mike had begun blowing her whistle each time. Her large brown eyes sparkled, she was having such fun, but the combination of noises was dreadful.

FWEEEEP! Br-r-r-ringg! FWEEEEP!

"This must be some new kind of torture," Mrs. Timmons remarked.

"Michelle, if you blow that whistle one more time, I swear I'll take it away from you!" Mr. Timmons advanced on Mike, who hastily tucked the whistle inside her blouse.

Rusty whispered into the phone, "Timmons' Total Service." Who'd have guessed there'd be so many calls?

"Is this Rusty Timmons?" said the voice on the phone.

"Yessir. Can we help you?"

"Probably. Anyone who can advertise like you has to be a good businessman."

"Thanks. You saw the signs, then."

A short laugh, more like a bark, answered him. "Boy, everyone has seen those signs! And we need workers here. We're new in town, but we've got an old place. We need help in the yard, in the cellar, in the house, all over. I want your oldest and best people—four ought to do it. People who can do the job right. What do you say?"

Rusty blinked at the amount of work being suggested. Even though the man on the phone sounded difficult, it would be worth it. "Well," he said, by way of beginning.

"Can I have the workers or not?" snapped the man.

Stung by the voice, Rusty said, "Sure, sure! I was just running over in my mind, trying to decide who'd be good for the job."

"Don't bother me with that. Just get them here. And I want *you* here to supervise. I only deal with the people at the top."

Rusty couldn't imagine who the man was. He knew no one who talked like this. "You do live in town, don't you?"

"Of course. The name's Smeltzer. Arnold Smeltzer. I'm in advertising myself. That's why I appreciated your signs. Now let me tell you when to work."

Rusty listened to the voice and wished he had never heard it. Smeltzer. Tiffany's father. And he would be working there while she and Dan . . .

"What do you say to that?"

"Excuse me?"

"Pay attention! I said that the four of you should come in the afternoons. That way Mrs. Smeltzer and my daughter can sleep late in the mornings. Summer vacation, you know. I'll meet you here at one tomorrow and we'll plan the work. Some has to be done by professionals, of course, but I like to see kids earn money. Tiffany

tells us you're a real smart boy, so I'm counting
on you, son." Now Mr. Smeltzer was sounding
folksy, as though he were an old friend. Already
Rusty disliked him.

"Tomorrow. One o'clock," Rusty said, trying to
sound and feel businesslike. After all, who said
you liked all of your customers? This was business, not some game. Slowly he hung up the
phone. He stared at the job chart and made himself think about business. Who should go with
him to the Smeltzers'?

"Who was that?" Mr. Timmons, who had been
writing bills at the table, looked up from his
checkbook.

"Smeltzer. Arnold Smeltzer. They bought the
old McFarland place out by school."

"And they want kids to fix it up?"

"Just some things. Yard and basement mostly.
He called it the *cellar.*"

Rusty's dad nodded, face sober. "I want you to
get the terms of your agreement in writing. Is
that clear?"

"Why?"

Mr. Timmons fiddled with his checkbook.
"Just that we don't know those people yet.
They're not from this area . . . and he's already

owing money around town a few places."

"He doesn't *pay* people?"

"Not exactly. The other merchants say he's got a lot of money, but he's slow to pay. I'd hope he wouldn't do kids that way, but just to be sure, you make him write up a contract. And think about it beforehand so you get a fair deal. Give him a list of what your jobs are worth per hour, so that he'll know."

Solemnly Rusty nodded. He liked hearing bad things about Mr. Smeltzer. He had sounded nasty enough on the phone. His dad didn't seem to like him either, and his dad liked everybody.

Rusty turned back to his study of the Service chart. Maybe Ruthann would want more work? Of course she would, although he dreaded spending every afternoon with her. But she'd be a match for Arnold Smeltzer. Rusty grinned as he imagined Ruthann and Tiffany's father in an argument.

"Russ?"

"Yeah, Dad?"

"Take a break and go for a swim. I'll send any calls over to Ruthann's house."

6

The Biggest Contract

Monday morning Rusty yawned and shifted position contentedly in bed. Eight-thirty, and no one had phoned. No Ruthann either. After his swim the night before, he had called the Howards and passed Mrs. Wayland's dog-walking job over to Marty. The manager of Timmons' Total Service was going to be busy enough at the Smeltzers' place. In only *two days*, Rusty thought, he had built a thriving business.

Lying on his back, hands under his head, Rusty decided that it would probably be okay to work at Tiffany's house. It was a joke, really. There he'd be, right under Dan's nose, and Dan would never guess the real reason—their basketball court. "Now that," his English teacher would say, "is irony." Only Julia knew the truth, and Rusty could trust her to keep the secret. He'd let Debbie think he was saving up for a car. Great cover. He grinned to himself.

And when Dan saw how much money the workers were earning at the Smeltzers', he'd want to be part of the crew. Then again, he might not. If Dan and Tiffany played right in front of them, it wouldn't be so funny. Nah, Rusty decided. No point in dreaming up something to worry about like his mother always did.

Rusty dressed and ambled downstairs. While he ate breakfast he could check the job chart and make sure everything was recorded correctly. Midway through his Cheerios, Ruthann knocked at the back door and entered. She was slapping dust from her jeans and shirt.

"Stupid pony!" She flopped into a chair. "Did Jermy Johnson get to you yet?"

"Yeah. Thanks a heap," he answered sarcastically as he put two pieces of bread in the toaster. "He can't work for me."

"He's a Grade-A turkey," Ruthann agreed.

"He can be a turkey somewhere else. Here. Have a piece of toast. Do you have any jobs for the chart?"

Ruthann nodded and entered the name of a

ninth-grade girl into the Friday slot. "All-day sitting job. She likes working alone." She looked up from the chart and grinned proudly.

Rusty chewed his toast and thought that she had a nice face when she smiled. "Those posters you made for the meal service already got them a job."

While Ruthann ate, Rusty told her about the job at the Smeltzers'. She grabbed at the chance to be part of the work crew.

"It's going to be hard work," he said.

"Who cares? How about Debbie Purdy? She's not afraid of work. Same for Bob Matthews."

"I was thinking about Bob, but I didn't know who else. Shouldn't it be a boy?"

"I don't know why! Girls're as good as boys!"

Rusty closed his eyes and waited for the barrage, but she said nothing more. When he opened one eye, she was still glaring at him. "Okay, okay. Debbie's fine," he said finally. "We're supposed to be at Smeltzers' at one, and we better take some tools, just in case he wants us to start on the yard or something."

At one, Rusty rang the bell beside the tall, weathered door of the old McFarland house. Now the Smeltzers' house, though it would be

years before anyone in Hampshire thought of it
that way.

"Place's a mess, by God," Ruthann observed.
Standing behind her on the steps were Debbie
and Bob.

The door opened. "Right on the dot. Come in
and we'll lay out the work." A short, heavy man
with a grating voice that Rusty recognized led
them down the hall toward a bright kitchen full
of new appliances and cupboards. It wasn't anything like the Timmons kitchen.

"We're fixing things up around here," Mr.
Smeltzer said loudly. He gestured from dish-
washer to microwave to gleaming metallic sur-
faces. "And you people will be a big part of it all."
The palsy-folksy tone of voice had returned, and
Rusty was glad his own dad never acted that
way.

Mr. Smeltzer ticked off on his fingers the jobs
he wanted done. "First, shape up the lawn and
hedges, and keep them that way. The lawn needs
seeding as well as fertilizer. The cellar has to be
sorted, because of the moving boxes, then
cleaned and painted. Floor needs painting, too.
All the flower beds have to be weeded, and I want
them weed-free the rest of the summer. Several

small trees out back need chopping down, and those stumps should be dug out. Then you can seed those places for grass. There's work in the orchard, too, but we can talk about that later."

He paused, forehead wrinkled in concentration. "Three outbuildings need the old paint scraped off and fresh paint put on. Two coats of new paint. They have to be cleaned out first, I guess, to get rid of the junk. That ought to do for starters." Eyeing Rusty, he jammed his hands in his pockets and rocked back on his heels.

"Ooooeee," Ruthann whistled low.

"We'll need to write that down, sir." Rusty's hands clenched behind his back, but he smiled pleasantly at Mr. Smeltzer. "We work by contract. Then you don't get a bad shock when we give you the bill." He forced an even wider smile.

"What?" barked Mr. Smeltzer. His dark-browed frown caused his eyes to scrunch up and nearly disappear. *"Contracts?"*

"Surely you're used to working by contract," Ruthann said coolly.

Mr. Smeltzer's head swung in her direction. "Who're *you*?"

"I'm the best worker you'll ever get, and at the best price." She turned to Rusty and asked in a professional voice, "Do you have a list of our job prices for Mr. Smeltzer to see?"

"Sure," Rusty replied. He reached into his pocket for the price list. Everyone in his group was standing at attention, like privates being grilled by their drill sergeant. Everyone except Ruthann, who leaned nonchalantly against a counter and gazed at Mr. Smeltzer unafraid. Just like I thought, Rusty said to himself, wanting to laugh out loud.

Rusty let Tiffany's father read the list. Then he said, "You keep the price list. Each week I'll write down how many hours were spent on each job, with the price totals for the week. You sign it, and I'll sign it, and we'll each have a copy."

Mr. Smeltzer looked up from his list. "If you insist. But I'd better not catch any of you fooling around, wasting my time and money. Understand?"

Ruthann spoke before Rusty had a chance. "We've heard they do that out East, where you come from, but not in Hampshire. If you'd lived here longer you'd know that."

Rusty cleared his throat. "If you check around, you'll see that our prices are better than anyone else's. And we *don't* fool around on the job. Sir."

Into the difficult silence that followed, feet came dashing down the hall. "Dan's mom is on the phone, Daddy, and she wants to know when we'll be home." Tiffany stopped when she saw the kitchen filled with her classmates. "Hi," she said. "Dan, some of Rusty's kids are here," she called back over her shoulder. "I'm so excited," she said to Rusty. "We're going to Cincy to a party to meet the baseball players. They know my father."

"Well, we're going to mow lawns," Bob said. "You eat a hot dog for me, okay?" He did not sound friendly, and Tiffany's face lost its brightness.

"You tell Dan's mother we're leaving at six and will be home by midnight," Mr. Smeltzer said to Tiffany. "You two run along now and have fun." He smiled broadly at Tiffany and Dan, who was now in the doorway with her.

"Hi," Dan said.

"Hi," Rusty replied, feeling awkward.

"Hot, huh?" Dan asked him. "Bet your pool feels good."

"Sure." Rusty remembered how many days he and Dan had spent in the pool. How Dan had made up a dive they called The Banana. They had needed different kinds of dives, because four feet isn't really enough water for diving.

"How's this for the first week?" Mr. Smeltzer held out a paper for Rusty to see. "You put the price per hour by each job, and then we'll see."

Rusty read the list for the first week. It covered only a fraction of the work Tiffany's father had suggested, and he knew that many weeks of work lay ahead. He wrote the price per hour for each job, not knowing how long the jobs would take. "I tried to be fair," he said, handing back the contract. "Same prices as on the list I gave you."

Mr. Smeltzer snorted as he studied the two papers. "You talk sassy, but you don't charge much," he concluded. "If you finish by the end of July, I'll give each of you a bonus. My wife wants to have a garden party early in August." He pulled a gold ballpoint pen from his shirt pocket and signed the contract. Then Rusty wrote his name, folded up the contract, and put it in his pocket.

"Let's get to work," Rusty said.

"Dan, let's go. We'll just be in the way," Tiffany urged. "And Brandy's lonesome. He's not sure he likes it here yet."

"That's Champagne's brother," Dan explained to Bob and Debbie and Ruthann as they all walked toward the front door. "He's a palomino, too. Came from the same horse farm in Kentucky."

"Whoop-de-dee," Ruthann said, but softly.

"That wasn't very nice." Tiffany's dark eyes flashed anger at both Ruthann and Rusty.

Coldly Ruthann said, "I'm *not* nice. Anyway, I work out with a real circus pony who does tricks!" She yanked open the front door and jumped down the steps to the lawn mowers they had brought.

Still frowning, Tiffany followed her down the steps. She started to say something, but the roar of the mower motor drowned her out. Ruthann turned the mower with a flourish, spraying Tiffany with grass.

That Monday afternoon on the old McFarland property was a hard one. The yard and shrubs had been ignored for so long that they were badly overgrown. Hedges fought being trimmed back for the mowers to reach the tough, weedy grass underneath. The motors on the mowers strained with effort, and sweat poured off the workers in constant streams. It seeped into every bit of their clothing, making them look as awful as they felt. They itched, their eyes burned from the perspiration and they kept on working.

Every now and then, Rusty looked up to see Dan cantering on Brandy. Dan jumping Brandy. Dan drinking something cold, no doubt, from tall, frosty glasses, in the shade with Tiffany.

At five-thirty, Rusty and Ruthann helped to clean the two mowers and the pruning shears. Each worker was filthy, soggy and discouraged. Cleaning up this old property was going to be worse than they had thought.

"Going to meet some real baseball players," mimicked Bob in a skinny voice. "They know my daddy. Oooooh." He wiped the seat of his lawn tractor as the work crew laughed with him.

"She oughta go back to New York," Ruthann said, blowing a puff of wet, sandy-colored hair off her forehead. "Anybody else would've given us something cold to drink."

"Holy crud, yeah!" Bob agreed. "All we had was the hose!"

"They're not all like that." Debbie borrowed Rusty's T-shirt from his back pocket and used it to wipe her face. "My aunt who works in a TV station is from New York, and she's super. I'm named after her." She stuffed the shirt back in Rusty's pocket.

"Today was the worst, I'll bet," Rusty said, wanting to keep the crew happy. "Tomorrow won't be so bad."

"Oh yeah?" Ruthann retorted, scratching a bug bite on her leg.

The workers headed for home, Ruthann keeping Rusty company until the turnoff for her street.

"I didn't know the pony did tricks," Rusty said to her as they walked.

She smiled without humor. "He does tricks all right."

"You been thrown a lot?"

"I just started, so how can it be a lot?"

"We ought to get somebody else to do it, some kid who knows horses."

"Over my dead body."

"That's what I'm afraid of," Rusty said, only half joking.

"He's going to know me pretty soon. Then it'll be easy."

"What's his name? You're always calling him *he*."

She hesitated. "Mr. Langendorfer wants to think up a good name for him. Got any ideas?"

Rusty stopped walking. "He has to have a name already—from the circus. What is it?"

"Hitler," Ruthann said, making a face. "Isn't that a riot? You can see why we need a new name."

"You shouldn't go there anymore." He made his voice sound as managerial as possible. "He can get somebody else to exercise that horse."

"No he can't. It's five dollars a day for an hour's work. And horse riding is fun. Just ask Tiffany."

"It sounds dangerous. We could be sued. So you *shouldn't go there*."

"You can't tell me what to do! *I'm* not going to sue anybody! Like I said, *nobody* tells *me* what to do!" Ruthann's eyes narrowed and she breathed deeply. At her corner, she turned away from Rusty and headed off down the street. She didn't say good-bye; she just walked away, head high.

Okay, he thought, if that's the way she wants it. Nothing was worth making such a fuss over. He'd be darned if he'd mention the pony again. She could think up her own name for the horse and he didn't need to know.

By the time supper was over, Rusty felt better. If he continued to work the way he had all afternoon, Ruthann would never think of calling him Chubsie again.

"Man, did we work today," he told his family. "Put in sixteen hours total for the four of us. Two-fifty an hour apiece. That's forty dollars!"

"He's turning into a dollar sign," Julia said.

"A dirty dollar sign," Mrs. Timmons agreed. "How about a shower and a swim?"

"Okay. Julia, did you get any calls for the Service this afternoon?"

"Of course. Four of them. Your business is unreal." She passed him a slip of paper with four names and phone numbers. "I ought to get a commission as your secretary, but I'll do it as a favor because I'm such a fantastically good sister."

"And modest, too," Rusty said, grinning. Just then the phone rang. "Timmons' Total Service. Rusty here."

"Hi. It's me. Rotten Ruthann."

Rusty didn't know what to say. He agreed with her . . . and he didn't. She was the best worker he had. And now she was apologizing in her own way. "Hello, Rotten."

"Did you get any more calls?"

"Yeah, four." He looked down at the paper his sister had given him. "But I don't know the names."

"I'll come over and see if I do. We can give people better workers if we know who they are and what they're like."

It wasn't long before Ruthann came through the Timmons back door. Rusty had listed the day's work at the Smeltzers' on the record sheet he planned to present Mr. Smeltzer at the end of their first week. He had recorded the same information on the giant worker chart by the phone. Just looking at those lists made him feel great. His was a *real* business.

"Phew!" Ruthann said, standing beside him to admire the worker chart. "Why'd it have to get hot just when we started work? Let's see those new people's names." She scanned the list.

"I do know these people," she said. "I'll call them from my place."

"Good. I'd rather go swimming." Rusty remembered his manners. "Wouldn't you like to swim? It feels great, you know." He watched her face and could see that she was tempted. This time she didn't refuse right away.

"Guess not. I don't have a suit anyway."

"You could borrow one of Julia's old ones. She's not much taller than you and almost as skinny."

"You've got a real way with words."

He laughed. "Sorry. I'll go ask Julia." On his way upstairs Rusty wondered why she didn't have a suit. Were the Millers that poor? Or was she afraid of the water? He couldn't remember ever seeing her at the rock quarry outside town where all the kids went to swim. But he couldn't imagine her being afraid of anything.

Back downstairs, he tossed a red bathing suit into her lap. "Julia said she's too tall for it and you can keep it."

"I *love* red!" Ruthann stood up, holding the suit against her chest. "Where can I change?"

"You take the bathroom down here, off the hall. It has a dinky shower in it. Mom doesn't let us swim if we're grubby." He smiled apologetically.

In the pool, Rusty sank down into a crouch so that his head was barely above water. Ruthann sat on the redwood decking that surrounded the pool, skirling her feet in the water, scooping up arcs of it that glinted in the evening sun. She cupped her hands to carry the water to her lap, and watched as it ran down her legs.

"Come on in. It feels terrific."

"How deep is it?"

"Just four feet all over. We wanted a real one, in the ground, but Mom couldn't afford it. This's fine, though. Look, here's one of the dives Dan and I like best." Rusty jumped out of the pool, leaped off the side, and curled up into a tight ball before he hit the water. It made a loud noise and a huge splash that lapped water across the decking.

"That's great," Ruthann said, but she didn't sound convinced. She descended the pool ladder slowly. "Oh, yeah. I forgot to tell you Jermy Johnson called me during supper. He wants to know when we're going to get him a job."

Rusty groaned and Ruthann grinned at him. "Pride of Ohio. Hangs right in there, doesn't he?"

7

Counting the Money

Rusty yawned with tiredness and made himself stay with the long column of figures. Even though he was beat, he was happy. The longer the column, the more money he was making.

Across the table Ruthann was also adding numbers. Her columns were shorter, each showing the jobs and earnings of a worker for the Service. "Have Molly and Lynn Gail been sitting every day?" she asked, looking up.

"I'm not sure," he said, yawning again. "We've been at Smeltzers' so much I can't keep track."

"Well, I think they owe you money. You'll have to ask them."

"There you go again."

"It's *your* business and *your* commissions! I'm not arguing, and I'm not managing anything. I just say they owe you money!"

"Okay, okay." He sighed. He had been in business slightly over two weeks, and it had been good but incredibly busy. He sure wasn't bored. Unfortunately, he was tired at night and didn't feel like playing flashlight tag or capture the flag or any of the summer nighttime games he used to play. Overall, though, he was satisfied. Timmons' Total Service was doing more business than even he had imagined. Whenever he left for the Smeltzers' or hung up his pruning shears in the garage, he'd see the place where the basketball court was going to be. He'd picture the shiny metal pole and the sparkling white backboard behind the hoop. It would be perfect. Dan would want to be there.

"You'll check with Molly and Lynn Gail, okay?" persisted Ruthann.

"Sure, sure," he replied, but he couldn't imagine that any workers would deliberately cheat him. "Both weeks have been about the same," he said, wanting to think about the good part. "About three hundred dollars' worth. Not counting Smeltzer. That's awesome! I get fifty dollars a week at Smeltzers', just like you—well, we'll get it when the job's done—and I'm banking thirty more every week from the Service commission."

"We earn it," Ruthann said darkly, massaging her back.

Rusty heartily agreed. He wondered if her back was sore from the yard work or from riding the pony. One evening he had gone to look at Mr. Langendorfer's horse. As Shetlands went, Hitler was the handsomest black-and-white pony Rusty had ever seen. And one of the biggest. But when the pony turned to look at him, Rusty had drawn back instinctively. Hitler had rushed the fence where Rusty leaned, and the sound of his hooves was menacing. He had whinnied shrilly and bumped his heavy, short shoulders against the fence as Rusty backed away. When he walked home that night, Rusty didn't think that renaming Hitler was going to help.

"Look at this," Ruthann said, interrupting his thoughts. She waved a strip of iridescent material in the air. "Your mom said I could have the other bathing suit Julia's outgrown. And it's my second-favorite color." She put the kelly-green suit back in her lap. "Let's hurry up so we can have time in the pool."

Rusty was sure by now that she'd never learned to swim. Her head hadn't been near the water on the few nights they'd gone swimming after supper. "I taught Mike to swim myself," he offered.

Ruthann ignored him. She bent her head to the column of figures and mumbled her addition aloud.

The next time they talked about business was a week later as they were weeding at the Smeltzers'. "You ask Molly and Lynn Gail about that money yet? Gramma says they're at Bentons' every day sitting those kids."

Rusty put down his trowel and sat back on his heels. He had checked the account books, which showed that Molly and Lynn Gail had a job at the Bentons' every other day. The job chart said the same thing. In his mind, he could picture the writing. "They're cheating, then," he admitted slowly. "Your gramma's sure?"

She nodded and went on weeding. "I hated all those spiders," she said, changing the subject, "but it was lots cooler working down in their basement."

"Yeah. When do you think they'll open all those boxes?" Rusty pushed the Molly–Lynn Gail problem to the back of his mind.

"They must've moved a lot. Those boxes don't look like they were opened in between. What does Mrs. Hoity-Toity do, anyway?"

"Sleeps," Rusty answered with a smile. "In the morning at least. In the afternoon she goes out."

"Hey, you guys, how's it going?" A different voice joined the conversation.

"Dan!" Rusty stood up. "Hi. How's it going with you?"

"Okay. Tiffany's practicing now. She has to get back at it, she said, for the rest of the summer." Dan looked at the ground and drew a design with the toe of his sneaker in the grass. He watched the design disappear as the grass blades stood erect again. "She plays the piano for concerts. Did you know that?"

"No," Rusty and Ruthann said together. "You kidding?" Ruthann added.

Dan shook his head. "She's been doing concerts for two or three years now. She just told me, but I guess she's really something. She even studied in Europe one year. And she says I can't listen to her practice. Makes her nervous."

"You haven't heard her?" Rusty asked.

"Nope. But they moved here because she was sick. Too many concerts, her dad said. She didn't practice at all for a long time. But she's better now, so she has to practice again. Every day." Dan sounded lost.

"Tut, tut," Ruthann said. "How pitiful for you." She continued to jerk weeds out of the flower bed.

Unable to help himself, Rusty laughed. Count on Ruthann, he thought. But the laugh died when he saw Dan's face. "Come on. It's just a joke." He smiled at his old friend.

"I don't see why you don't like her!" Dan flared. "Just because she's got money is no reason to hate her."

"Geez, Dan," Rusty protested, his hands held out. "I don't hate *anybody.*"

"Well *I* do," announced Ruthann. "She wouldn't be friends with me if her life depended on it."

"Come on, Ruthann, don't fight, okay?" Rusty turned from Dan to Ruthann and back to Dan.

"I'll fight whenever I *feel* like it!" She tossed a weed behind her as she grubbed furiously under a thorny bush. "And quit telling me what to do!"

Rusty looked at Dan. "Done anything exciting lately?"

Dan's face cleared. "Yeah! I've been to two Reds games already. Her dad's company's got a box, and it's super." His eyes shone. "I love baseball, and here I am, going to games all the time. Lucky, huh?"

Rusty ached to tell Dan something about another favorite game. How they would both have a new place to play basketball very soon. But it wasn't the right time.

"We're really making a business here," Rusty said instead. "I get thirty dollars a week in commissions, plus fifty from this job."

"Wow!" Dan looked respectfully at Rusty. "Do you still have room for me?" he asked, voice low.

"Sure! Always."

"You know how to work?" Ruthann glanced up from her pile of weeds.

Dan started to say something, then closed his mouth. "I can work as good as you can" was all he said seconds later.

"Okay." Ruthann stood up. "Let's go find where she's practicing." Back erect, she set off for the house.

"No, we can't!" Dan rushed after her, waving

his hands in the air, shaking his head no, his whole body a moving negative. "She'll have a fit!"

Ruthann turned. "You afraid of her?"

A few minutes later, the three of them were crouched below a long window shuttered against the afternoon sun. For the Smeltzers, air conditioning had been built into the old McFarland house. All the windows were closed tightly. But even through the window, piano music came clearly.

"I'll be double-damned!" Ruthann said after a time. "She really can play that thing!"

Rusty remembered noticing Tiffany's long hands. They must be the reason she could make such big chords and powerful sounds. It was really something, just as Dan had thought. Rusty had never heard a piano up close making such sounds.

"*Mister* Timmons!"

Guiltily, everyone jumped. Rusty felt his heart making awful thumps in his chest. "I'm sorry, Mr. Smeltzer. It . . . it was so wonderful we couldn't leave. We won't do it again. Promise."

Tiffany's father barked his short laugh. "Stick with it and you may be a politician someday.

Look, get back to work and we'll forget it. I came looking for you because you've got a phone call. Go in the back door and take it in the kitchen." He turned from Rusty to Dan.

"Well, son, couldn't stand it, eh? Had to hear her." He put his arm around Dan's shoulders, and together they walked away, talking.

"El Creepo," Ruthann whispered, gesturing at Mr. Smeltzer.

Rusty nodded agreement. "I'll be right back," he told her, wondering about the phone call.

What he heard from Julia was enough to send him back outdoors on the run. "Got to hurry. Some problem about Molly and Lynn Gail at Bentons' house. Take my wagon with the tools, okay?"

8

The Pinch of Shining Armor

"You'd better call now, because when they phoned here a few minutes ago they were hysterical. That's why I called you. Here's the number." Julia handed him a slip of paper and went back outside to her towel in the sun.

Rusty dialed the number and tried to imagine why Molly Lemon and Lynn Gail Cleary would be hysterical. "Hello, Molly? Lynn Gail?"

"Rusty?" began Lynn Gail's voice, all quivery.

"Tell him we're stuck in here, Lynn Gail!" screamed Molly's voice in the background. "You kids open that door this minute, you hear?"

"They locked us in," Lynn Gail said. "You've gotta come quick and get us out because we can't!

The windows're stuck, too!" She broke down and sobs took over. "Rusteee," she wailed.

Rusty heard more crying, a scuffle and "Give me the phone!" Then Molly's voice came pouring into his ear. "Look here, Rusty, *we've had it*! Get over here and get us out before some kid burns this house down."

Insanely, Rusty felt the urge to laugh. *Two* sitters and *still* the little kids had— Then he thought, What if they did burn the house down? "How many Benton kids are there?"

"Five!" Molly hollered into his ear. "And we can't just sit here and talk on the phone! I mean, *really*!"

"I just wondered," Rusty said weakly. "Be right there." He hung up, and as he did he realized that he didn't know where the Bentons lived. Had to be close to Ruthann, he decided. Her gramma said she saw the girls every day. And they're cheating, he remembered.

Rusty bolted down the sidewalk toward his bike in the garage. "Going to Bentons'," he called out to Julia as he got on his bike. "The kids locked Molly and Lynn Gail in."

"I'll bet they did." Julia sat up on her towel and gave him her full attention. "You be careful.

That one kid, Wolfy Benton, is supposed to be a piece of work. My Y.E.S. sitters won't go there." She stood up and shook out her towel. "Call me if you have trouble."

"Thanks a lot." He smiled gratefully at her as he pedaled out of Holly Tree Court, then across Grove and up toward Willow Avenue, where Ruthann lived way down at the end of the street. The Bentons' would have to be nearby. What am I going to do when I get there? he asked himself. How old was Wolfy Benton? And what kind of name was that anyhow? Like Hitler. Who could be good with names like that?

A white mailbox with "Wm. J. Benton, 40 Willow Ave." printed on it told Rusty he had arrived. He pedaled past the mailbox and swooped up the narrow driveway. He still didn't know what he was going to do.

Rusty peered into the garage and saw a door. He figured it led into the kitchen, like most doors on the insides of garages. He put his ear against it and listened. Nothing. His hand turned the doorknob slowly. Maybe the kids were watching TV, and he could sneak in and unlock the door that Molly and Lynn Gail were behind.

Carefully Rusty pushed open the door and

looked inside. Normal kitchen, he thought. Now he could hear low voices and background music, like a TV or radio in another room. All worked up for nothing, he told himself as he stepped into the kitchen.

"YA-HAAAAA!" shrieked a voice. Its source leaped out from behind the door and began squirting water all over him.

"Hey, stop! Come on!" Rusty yelled as he put up hands to try to defend himself. But the kid could really shoot. He had two pistols going full speed, and Rusty was dripping. Smelly water, he thought. Like real strong perfume.

Finally, he pushed through the streams of it to the person with the pistols. After a struggle, he grabbed one pistol and began shooting back.

Zap! Got his ear! Rusty grinned with satisfaction as he took aim at the kid's other ear. Must be Wolfy. Boy, can he shoot. Rusty dodged a stream aimed at his face. "You Wolfy?" he asked, crouching behind a kitchen chair for protection.

"How'd you know?" The Wolfy person was skinny and dirty. He looked about seven.

"Just a lucky guess." Rusty smiled around the chair at Wolfy. "You're some shot. We ought to call you Kid Benton. But this stuff smells—and

so do *I* now. What is it?"

"Chanel Number Five," Wolfy replied. He stopped shooting. "It's Mom's favorite. Who're you?"

Rusty's mind reeled. Once, on Julia's orders, he and Mike had given up a whole month's allowance to help Julia buy a birthday present for their mother. That present had been a tiny bottle of Chanel Number Five.

"That stuff costs a fortune," Rusty croaked. He stood up and walked over to Wolfy. "Here. I'll help you put it back in the bottle, okay?" Surprisingly, Wolfy agreed, but when they had finished, the bottle was nearly empty. And it had been a big bottle.

"Let's put it back," Rusty suggested. "Does your mom keep it on her dresser?"

Wolfy looked away. "Yeah, I'll do it later. Wanna play in the hose with me?"

So they're in the parents' room, Rusty concluded. No wonder they had a phone to use.

"Hey, who *are* you? You wanna play in the hose?" Wolfy repeated.

"Uh, sure. You go turn on the sprinkler for us. I'll leave my clothes in the john and be right out."

Wolfy went out the door and Rusty made a fast search of the Bentons' house. At the end of a long hallway, one door seemed about right. He pushed on it and it was locked. "Lynn Gail? Molly?"

"Rusty? Is that you?" Molly's voice was edgy.

"Rusteee? Hurry up!" Lynn Gail sounded as if she would cry again any minute.

"Why's the lock on this side of the door?"

"Oh, Rusteeeee," Lynn Gail whimpered, "it's a new house, and maybe it was put on wrong. How should *we* know? Just hurry up."

"Where're all the other kids?" Rusty asked, frowning at the door lock. He felt in his pocket for something sharp or pointed.

"Look! *We're locked in, remember?* We don't know where *any* of the kids are!" Molly's voice was poisonous.

"Geez, Molly, I just asked. I'm trying! I came right away, didn't I?" He tried his bike lock key in the door, but it was too large. He needed something like an ice pick or a pointy awl. "Be right back."

"Hurreee." Lynn Gail's cry followed him down the hall.

Back in the Bentons' kitchen, Rusty jerked

open one drawer after another until he found one filled with string and small tools. He pawed through the stuff and discovered a short metal thing with a point.

"Whatcha doin' in my dad's drawer?"

Rusty turned to face him. "Well, Wolfy, it's like this. When I was in the john, I heard the toilet running. Tank stuck, you know? So I thought I'd do you a favor and fix it."

"Oh yeah? *Who are you anyhow*?" Wolfy tipped his head to one side and studied Rusty.

"Just a new kid in the neighborhood. Name's Rusty. I've got nothing to do," he said casually. "Go check our hose, okay? I'll be right out."

Wolfy nodded. "I'm new, too. We've only been here a few months. It stinks here." He went back outdoors.

Rusty raced back down the hall to the master bedroom. He was glad *he* had never had to move. "There sure are a lot of weirdos in town all of a sudden," he grumbled, thinking of Wolfy and the Smeltzers. He stuck the pointed tool in the lock and pushed till it gave way.

"It's about time," Molly greeted him as he poked his head into the room. "I was just about to call my dad!"

"Why didn't you, then? And you can get ready a *real* list of the days you both have been here, too. You think I like leaving work to come do this? Think I like getting soaked with Chanel Number Five? Holy crud!" Rusty had picked up "holy crud" from Bob Matthews, and he liked it, especially now.

Molly looked as if she'd been told off, and she was silent. Lynn Gail said, "Thanks a lot, Rusty. Did you see Susie or Sally? Or Robbie? Or the baby?" She sounded like her old self now that the door was standing open.

Rusty shook his head. "Let's go look for them."

They found the baby asleep in his crib. Lynn Gail closed the door to his room and led the search for the other children. None of them were in the house. "We'll have to make Wolfy tell us," Rusty said.

"Fat chance," snapped Molly.

"How about the toolshed out back?" Lynn Gail suggested. "Wolfy plays games in there with Robbie and the twins."

Rusty and the girls hurried out the kitchen door, through the garage and into the backyard. Rusty began to feel fear in his stomach. What if the rest of the kids weren't in the shed?

"Hey! You a friend of *theirs*?" The voice was Wolfy's. Angry and betrayed. "How'd you know where they were?" He came round the side of the house, pistols blazing.

"Cut that out, you little creep!" Molly put her hands over her face. "That stuff stings your eyes, Lynn Gail!"

"It's just water, ya big booby!"

"Come on! Stop it!" Rusty went over to stand by Wolfy. "It's just water now, right?"

Wolfy let the guns drop to his sides. "Yeah. You a friend of theirs?"

"We work together. Timmons' Total Service. I'm Rusty Timmons. Wolfy, we have to know where your brother and sisters are. I don't want to call the police."

"They're in here!" Molly called from beside the low toolshed. "Right where we thought. Tied to the lawn mower!" She left the window to the shed and came to stand in front of Wolfy. "Give me the key to the shed, you little creep, or I'm gonna tell your mom and dad when they get home."

"Stop callin' me a little creep!" Wolfy's voice was shrill. "I'll tell my mom you called me names again!"

"Wolfy? Please?" Lynn Gail held out her hand. "Robbie's crying. He knows you're his big brother. Remember what I said about big brothers?"

Wolfy looked down at the grass. "Okay. Let 'em out. I don't care." He took a key out of his pocket and gave it to Rusty.

Rusty opened the shed door and helped the sitters to untie Robbie, who looked about four, and the twins, Sally and Susie, two-year-olds who weren't upset at all. Rusty carried the twins into the house, and when Molly and Lynn Gail had gotten everyone a snack, he said he guessed he'd leave. "I, uh, I still need a real list of your working hours," he told Molly. She averted her eyes and nodded.

Outside, Rusty saw that Wolfy had turned on the sprinkler. Wearing his clothes and sneakers, Wolfy sat under it, alone. Rusty wheeled his bike close to the sprinkler, where a few welcome drops would fall on him. "You know Clint Carlsrud? He's just one block over. Kid about your age."

Wolfy blinked. "Clint lives on Hillside? Over there?"

"Yup. Big old yellow house. His brother's in my

grade. He said Clint's real tough. You'd like him. You tell him Rusty Timmons said your name was Kid Benton." Rusty grinned at him. " 'Bye. I have to get back to work."

Rusty hopped on his bike and made one circle around the yard before he left. "Must be hard— moving, I mean. You say hello to Clint 'n' his brother for me, Kid." He waved at Wolfy as he pedaled down the driveway.

By the time he got to his own driveway, Rusty felt twenty feet tall and growing. He knew he had made a friend of Wolfy. He had handled it well, the whole thing, even asking for Molly to turn in an honest list of their jobs. Dan had said he wanted to be part of the Service, *and* he had rescued two maidens in distress. Heck of a day.

When he got off his prancing steed, Rusty made a few swipes in the air with his trusty sword. "Aha! Stand aside, you dog!" Swiisssshhh! Swooosssshhh! The smooth cutting motions of the sword were beautiful to see.

Purposefully, Rusty sheathed his weapon and strode into the kitchen of his castle. He would arrange the evening's schedule and go for a swim in the moat.

"Hey? You paying attention?" Julia's voice crumbled the castle.

"What is it?" He looked at his sister, who held the phone receiver in her hand.

"He just hung up. It was Jermy Johnson. He's on his way over here. Is he working for you?" She hung up the phone.

"He keeps saying he's going to."

"Somebody said he was seeing a shrink. In Cincinnati."

"I haven't seen anything different about him."

"Maybe this is it. Needing to work with kids."

Rusty shrugged. "Well, not me. I don't have to, do I?"

Julia spoke carefully. "We let everybody sign up in the Y.E.S. office. I think it'd really hurt their feelings if we didn't. And it wouldn't be fair. We're a job service, not some club."

He sat down at the table. Was he running a club? He had told Ruthann it was a business. He *knew* it was a business. If he called back fast, maybe he'd catch Jermy at home. He could think of something to tell him on the phone, and then he wouldn't have to let him in the house.

Binnnggg, bonnnggg.

"That's him," Julia said. "Jermy's here."

Rusty stood up hastily. "Tell him I'm in the bathtub. That'll give me a chance to think." He raced up the steps to the second floor before Julia could tell him no.

He sat on the edge of the bathtub and ran cold water so that he sounded bathtubby—truthful. Although he wasn't sure why he cared what Jermy Johnson thought. He took off his sneakers and socks and stuck his feet into the cold tub, wiggling his toes under the pouring faucet. Nearly all the jobs had workers. Some of the kids who had signed up were too young for the jobs available. Others hadn't wanted to work unless it was fun and easy.

By now, the kids who were left had been matched up with jobs. Rusty had put off finding someone to work for old Mrs. Sheffield, a fussy, critical lady. She had phoned for a person to weed her flower and vegetable gardens twice a week. It would be hot, demanding work, and no one had wanted it.

"He can take it or leave it," Rusty said out loud. He turned off the tub faucet. "Keep his hands busy anyhow." He pulled his towel off the rack and dried his feet.

Downstairs, Rusty found Jermy standing in

the kitchen, looking out the window toward the pool. "I've only got one job left," Rusty said. "It's weeding for old Mrs. Sheffield."

Jermy turned from the window. "I'll do it. When do I go?"

"You really want it?"

Jermy nodded. Rusty saw then that Jermy was wearing bib overalls and that both hands were jammed deep in the pockets of the overalls. That's a change, he thought. "I'll call her now and ask when she wants you to come."

Rusty made arrangements with Mrs. Sheffield and told Jermy, "The Service gets ten percent. Everybody stops by once a week to pay."

"Fine. And thank you very much. How am I going to distinguish between weeds and flowers? Will she show me?"

"Haven't you ever weeded gardens?"

"Never." Jermy pushed his hands farther down into the overalls.

"You'd better ask Mrs. Sheffield, then. She's cranky. She'll be fussy about how it's done."

"That's okay. My folks are so particular about everything you wouldn't believe it. Thanks, Rusty." He walked over to the back door, nodded once and was gone.

Julia popped out from behind the dining room louvered doors. "That went great, Rusty. You did fine."

"He is different. He had his hands in his pockets the whole time," Rusty told her. "You know, we used to go right up to him and sing, 'It ain't how you pick your nose, it's where you put the booooogggger.' "

Julia shuddered. "That's revolting!"

Rusty grinned and turned to the telephone. "I have to check in with Ruthann to see what work they did at Smeltzers'. When're we eating supper?" He dialed the number as he spoke.

"Miller residence" came the soft, old voice in his ear.

"Hi, Gramma Miller," Rusty said. He had met Ruthann's grandmother only twice, but he was comfortable calling her Gramma. She was that sort of lady. "Can I talk to Ruthann, please?"

"She's with that pony again." Gramma Miller paused. "It isn't my business, and she'd eat me alive—"

Rusty heard a door slam in the background. Ruthann's voice intruded loudly into the conversation. "And no right to tell my private business. Give me the phone and *I'll* tell him! . . .

"Hi there. Rotten here. Did you see where I put your wagon?"

"Look, Rotten," Rusty said. "What's that pony doing?"

"Nothing special," she said airily. "But Gramma has never liked horses. Anyway, do you remember that our porch over here still needs painting? You can give that job to Jermy if you want. I don't care. But I can't talk now. We're going to the drive-in for chili dogs to celebrate. My mom's in town for a change. See you tomorrow." And the phone went dead.

9

Escape to Kentucky

Rusty lay in the sun by the pool. Two weeks had gone by without any real worries. Final grade cards had come at last, and he had gotten the grades he wanted, with a nice note from Mr. Ingram about the dolphin report. It had pushed his science grade up to an A– for the last marking period. An A on the math final had kept his year's average at A– in math. The other grades could be B's as far as he was concerned, just as long as his two favorite subjects stayed steady.

And work was going well, too. Not long ago Fred Jenkins' Rent-A-Cat, Bismarck, had been stuck in a tree at Ruthann's house, but that had been funny, not serious. The firemen had res-

cued Bismarck, been friendly about the whole
thing and gone on their way. "It's all Marty Howard's fault," Fred had told Rusty. "He can't con-
trol that mob of dogs he walks every day."

Rusty rolled over on his back with a contented,
lazy yawn. He peered down at his stomach and
couldn't even imagine the friendly roll that had
once been there. It was gone, and in its place
were muscles from the work he'd done at the
Smeltzers'. Only a couple of days ago Ruthann
had looked at the length of his jeans and said,
"You expecting a flood or something?" So he was
growing, too. Those jeans had been new in the
spring.

Best of all, he felt rich. His bank account held
$180.00 plus the ten he'd started with, for a total
of $190.00, and he hadn't been paid for working
at the Smeltzers' yet. He would have more than
necessary for the best basketball court around.

"Hot enough for you up there?"

Rusty sat up, squinting in the bright sunlight.
"Hey, Dan! Come on up."

Dan bounded up the steps. "Care if I go in?
This's too hot for me. I hate July." Without waiting for an answer, Dan stripped down to swim
trunks and dove into the water. He swam the

short length of the pool a few times, then hauled himself onto the deck beside Rusty. "That's better," he said, sighing and stretching out. "Got any more jobs for me yet? Tiffany practices every day, do you believe it? I'd go nuts."

"It'd be tough, all right." Rusty wondered if the pool was the only reason Dan had come over. That and wanting another job because Tiffany was busy. Then he shook himself mentally, amazed that he had thoughts like that about Dan.

Dan propped himself up on one elbow. "You know, I tried to talk Ruthann out of that pony job. I know a lot more about horses than she does, and she told me off, *but good.* Had a hissy right in the middle of Center Street where everybody could see. And she'll say *anything*! I don't see how you stand her every day."

Rusty turned away to hide a smile. He could imagine the scene Ruthann had created in downtown Hampshire. When he thought about it, though, he was on her side. Where had Dan been when the Service got started? Not available, that's for sure. Ruthann had worked with the pony for weeks, so why would she just hand over the job to someone else?

"She works really hard," he told Dan. "Bob and Debbie like her a lot, too."

"Huh!" Dan snorted. "She could try acting like a girl for a change."

In his mind Rusty saw Ruthann's face when he'd given her Julia's old red bathing suit. "She's her own kind of girl," he said, eager to change the subject. "Let's go inside and check the job chart. We always get calls on Sundays, and kids leave on vacation. I'll bet we find something. One mowing job isn't enough, I know."

Inside, they consulted the chart. "Here," Rusty said, pointing to Tuesday mornings. "Craig Van Hoff's going on vacation for two weeks and can't do yard work at Wilsons'. You can take his place. That's a good job, too. Craig gets a dollar tip every Tuesday. Workers keep all the tips," he reminded Dan.

"Great! I'll write down the name and address."

Just then the phone rang. "Maybe something else for you right here," he said as he picked up the receiver.

The caller was Mrs. Sheffield. She started in talking at Rusty and when she wound up she said, "And I've never had a nicer person on the place. I'm calling Jeremy's parents, too, but I thought you'd like to know. Your service is a good idea, Rusty. Good-bye now, but you be sure to tell that Howard boy to keep his dogs down your way, where they belong."

Dazed, Rusty hung up the phone and stood staring into space. Jermy Johnson was a success. Who'd have believed it?

Dan interrupted his musing. "Not a job for me, huh? Well, guess I'll be going. The Smeltzers are putting in a pool—did I tell you that? The builders can't start till late August, but it'll be done in September. They've got the brochures now, and Tiffany said I could help decide on the tile and all. Sure would be nice to have that much money." Dan thanked Rusty for the swim and let himself out the back door.

Rusty moseyed outdoors to the pool, where the rest of the family was now enjoying Sunday. Last summer Dan had been part of that family group, but Dan had changed, he decided, not just grown taller.

"Now that's what I like to see," Mr. Timmons said as Rusty joined them by the pool. "The prosperous businessman taking a day off."

"About time," his mother added. "You've had a day like this coming, Rusty."

"He won't even let me see his bankbook," Mr. Timmons teased. "Probably afraid I'll ask him to pay room and board."

"The phone bill will do," Julia said dryly.

"You guys are just jealous." Rusty leaped into the pool, splashing water on all sides.

FWEEEEEP!

"Stop it, Michelle. You're wet anyway," her mother said mechanically. She turned to Rusty's father. "If you think you can get away from the store, we ought to grab a weekend at the folks' cabin. They'll be at the farm until sometime in mid-August, you know."

"Things are slow now, with people on vacation. How about next weekend? That okay with you kids?"

"I'll stay home," Rusty said regretfully, thinking of the walleyes he wouldn't catch this summer. There would be other summers at Kentucky's Lake Cumberland. "If Gramma and Grampa aren't there, they won't care whether I come or not. I can't leave the business."

"I want to go," Julia and Mike said simultaneously. Then there was a long silence. Rusty could tell his parents were deciding what to say next.

"Hey, come on! I love going to the lake, but it's a bad time. We have to finish at Smeltzers' before the first of August. And my business is great right now."

"You can't stay in town alone," Mrs. Timmons said.

"Your mother's right. Family vacations are important, too. Next year Julia will be in college and working every summer, not baby-sitting for us. This could be the last trip we take as a family."

Rusty looked from one parent to another. "What if people need workers? They're used to calling here!"

"*And* at Ruthann's," his dad said firmly. "Rusty, the subject is closed. For four days they can call Millers' house. I'm not going to argue about it."

Through the week that followed, Rusty tried to change his parents' minds so that he could stay home with his business. But things worked against him. Dawn and Priscilla, who had been running a smooth meal service for five customers, began to have problems.

"Rusty," Dawn said Monday on the phone, "could you help Pris deliver meals tonight? I don't feel so hot."

That night and the next, while Dawn was in bed with flu, Rusty helped Priscilla deliver all the meals. Somehow, he missed his own suppers and ended up with peanut butter sandwiches.

Bob Matthews told him Wednesday that he'd mowed the wrong lawn that morning and the people wouldn't pay him. That same afternoon at the Smeltzers' he mowed the hose and cut it into several small pieces. "Don't worry about it," Rusty said, sounding more cheerful then he felt. "Business expense, that's all. The Service will buy a new one and nobody'll ever know."

By Thursday, Dawn was up and Priscilla was down with the same flu bug. That evening, Rusty carted meals again to help Dawn, who still looked pale and tired. When he got home, Ruthann was waiting in the kitchen. "Just checking to see our charts agree," she said as he dragged in the door. "I'll help Dawn tomorrow and Saturday. Prissy'll be okay by Sunday."

Rusty nodded, grateful for her help. Ruthann would do fine without him. She'd made that clear earlier in the week when he'd explained about the Timmons' family vacation. Once she had told him she could do anything. By this time he believed her.

"All the commissions these four days will be yours," he said.

"Of course." Then she grinned. "But it'll be a pain in the butt to figure it out."

"I'll figure it out, Rotten."

"No calling names. This's *business*, remember?"

Later that evening, as he packed his suitcase for the lake, Rusty was perfectly content to leave his business. He helped his dad load boxes of groceries into the car and could hardly wait for the next morning. There were a few enormous old walleyes in the lake, and maybe this time he'd finally hook one of them.

"Looks like we're leaving for the month, not four days," Mr. Timmons commented as he tied the fishing poles to the top of the car.

10
August Dog Days

Monday night, when the Timmons family got home from Lake Cumberland, everyone was too tired to do anything but flop into bed.

Tuesday morning the phone began ringing. Marty Howard called first. He spoke to Mr. Timmons, who was making coffee in the kitchen.

The second call was Ruthann. She talked with Mrs. Timmons, who was unpacking leftover lake groceries.

The third call was Mr. Smeltzer, wondering why Rusty's crew wasn't finished. He talked to Mike, who said, "I'll go get him out of bed."

"I'm on upstairs, Mike," Rusty said sleepily. "Can I do something for you, Mr. Smeltzer?

Mike, hang up the phone." The downstairs phone receiver slammed into place and Rusty winced. "Sorry, sir. Mike's only seven."

Mr. Smeltzer said, "Rusty, when are you going to finish up here? My wife wants to have a garden party this weekend. You were supposed to be done by August first."

Rusty closed his eyes and concentrated. He wasn't sure, but he thought it was the thirtieth of July. "There are just two sheds left to paint, and some yard work. We'll finish by Friday night," he promised recklessly.

"All right. If you do, I'll still pay that bonus. I tried to call you all weekend, did you know that?"

"No, sir. We went on a family trip to Kentucky."

Mr. Smeltzer's laugh barked. "People running businesses don't take time off—didn't anyone ever tell you that? Well, see you this afternoon. Don't be late."

Rusty hung up and yawned back down the hall to his bedroom. First, he thought, I'll have some breakfast. A little bacon, maybe, and toast and orange juice. Maybe a bowl of Frosted Mini-Wheats. It wouldn't be as good as the walleyed pike he'd caught in the lake, of course. He pulled on his jeans and yanked an old T-shirt over his head.

"Russell?? Would you come downstairs, please?" Mr. Timmons' voice filled the stairwell and the hall and Rusty's room.

Something was wrong. Rusty grabbed his sneakers and headed for the kitchen. "What is it?" he asked as soon as he saw his parents.

"My pool" was all his mother could say. She took her handbag off the kitchen counter. "I'll be at the office if anyone needs me." She left the kitchen.

"Sit down, Rusty." His father didn't seem nearly as upset as his mother. Of course, that was normal. "While we were at the lake," Mr. Timmons said, "Marty Howard gave three dogs a flea-soap bath. Don't ask me why he had to do three at once."

Rusty nodded. He wouldn't ask.

"Anyway, they broke loose, ran across Grove and went for a swim in our pool. You should see it. Soap scum all over the top of the water. But there's only one rip in the liner that I can find, so it isn't too bad."

Rusty put his head in his hands.

Hastily, Mr. Timmons said, "It wasn't *your*

fault, Rusty! And your mother's more upset than she would be if she weren't tired. We shouldn't have stayed as late as we did in Kentucky, and I know we're all tired. But we can easily repair the pool liner if we drain the water. Marty said he'd do all the work if we'd just tell him what to do."

Rusty looked up. "If we can't fix it so it's right, I'll buy a new liner. I have plenty of money."

"Let's not jump to conclusions. I started the pool on backwash and it's pumping out now. When it's empty, we'll see what it needs." He slipped on his suit coat. "Sometimes it's rugged getting back into the swing of things after a few days off." He smiled. "You're supposed to call Ruthann. See you tonight."

After his dad left, Rusty sat at the table. He put off calling Ruthann for fear she would have bad news, too. Eventually he left the kitchen and went outdoors to look at the pool.

He climbed the few steps to the deck and knelt by the edge to stare down into the scummy receding water.

"It stinks, too, if you put your nose close." Mike's voice startled him.

Rusty looked up to see her kneeling beside him on the deck. She must have followed him outside. He hadn't even heard her. "Thanks," he said glumly. "Thanks a bunch."

Mike bent her head and slipped off the dark-blue cord that held the policeman's whistle. "Here. Blow. It helps a lot."

Astounded, Rusty put out his hand and took the whistle. He had never seen her take it off before. No one else had ever blown that whistle.

"Go on. Blow really hard."

Rusty blew, breathy at first, then hard. It made a terrible sound, as always, but she was right. Somehow it helped. FWEEEEP! FWEEEEEEP! FWEEEEEEP!

"For the Jeeezus Christ!" Ruthann shouted. "Shut that thing up!"

Mike sucked in her breath, horrified. "Good thing my dad isn't here!" she told Ruthann as she reached for the whistle.

Rusty looked down to the grass where Ruthann stood, hands on hips. Managing a smile, he said, "You seen this yet?"

"Last night, after Marty called me. He feels real bad. He should be here any minute."

"I don't remember what the commission is on his jobs, but I'll bet it isn't enough," Rusty said, turning his back on the pool.

Ruthann giggled. "Ain't that the truth!"

FWEEEEEP! Mike frowned at Ruthann.

Ruthann grinned at her. "That's the loudest whistle I ever heard. Where can I get one?"

"Can't," Mike replied smugly. "Only policemen and policewomen have them."

"And Michelle Timmons," added Rusty. "Come on, let's go inside. We can't do anything to fix it, not for a couple of days."

"Sure is hot," Ruthann said as they went toward the house. "I've never been tan like this. And my hair's getting blonder every day. See?" She held out a hank of silky, pale-gold hair.

Because he didn't like his own hair, Rusty had learned to ignore the whole subject. But now he looked at Ruthann's. "Yeah, it's nice. My mom said so the other night. She said models have it dyed to get it to look like that."

"Thanks," she said, tossing the lock of hair back over her shoulder.

That afternoon at the Smeltzers' the late July sun worked further on everyone's skin and hair. But this time it blazed down with almost unbearable heat. Within minutes of beginning work, everyone was drenched with sweat. Flies and gnats swarmed around them, adding to the misery. Around three o'clock Rusty needed a break. Telling Bob he'd be right back, he put his paint bucket aside and went to sit in the shade of the fruit trees that lined one edge of the property.

Ruthann joined him, and they agreed it was too hot to work. "Must be over a hundred," Rusty said, swatting at the gnats on his face and crawling into his ears. "My head hurts, and it never does that."

"Gramma said it was too hot. She said to tell Smeltzers we'd work evenings but not daytimes when it was this hot."

Rusty nodded. There wasn't even any air. Not a leaf moved. In the evening maybe a breeze would come up, and the terrible sun would go down.

After supper that night, he told his parents that his work crew was going back to the Smeltzers'. "We have to finish on Friday. Tiffany's mother is having a party this weekend. We'll quit when it's too dark to see."

Mrs. Timmons stopped watering houseplants and turned to him. "I should hope so! You'd better wear mosquito repellent, too." She filled her watering can and cooled her hands in the running water at the same time. "Every year we get a few killer days, but it's too bad you have to work in this heat. When you're finished there on Friday, that's it. He can hire a professional adult crew."

"Yeah," Rusty said thoughtfully. He wouldn't have agreed with her a few weeks ago, but now he did. "He even thinks we can prune his fruit trees. We don't know how to do that. Not right, anyway."

Mr. Timmons, who had been reading the newspaper, looked up at Rusty. "Absolutely not. No climbing in trees or on ladders. You remember what I said about dangerous jobs."

"Nothing is going to happen," Rusty said soothingly, refusing to think about all the painting they did using ladders. The phone rang, and he leaped for it, glad of the diversion.

"Hey, Mister Manager."

"Hi, Dan. How's it going?"

"Great! Mowed two lawns today. In the morning, before it got so awful hot. Did you know grass likes it hot? Long as it rains, I mean."

"Oh yeah?" Rusty looked at his watch.

"Yeah. Did you hear that Tiffany was giving a concert in Cincinnati? In November."

"Look, Dan . . ." Rusty began.

"You in a hurry?"

"We have to be at Smeltzers' now. Her mom's giving a party this weekend and they want all the work done."

"Wow. Well, look, I was calling to see if you can come to my party. My birthday's Thursday, remember? And Tiffany's dad said my family could have his company box that day for a ball game. So I can ask three people—besides my folks and brother."

"Three people," Rusty repeated dully.

"Yeah. You, and anybody else we want, and Tiffany. We have to leave for the ballpark before noon, and we're going out to supper on the way home, and be back about ten. If you're *around* Tiffany, you'll get to like her, I just *know* it."

"On Thursday?"

"Yeah! You deaf or something? What's the matter?"

"I can't go. We're just barely going to finish at Smeltzers' as it is. Working as much as we can every day. I can't go."

There was a silence at Dan's end of the phone. Finally he said, "Geez, Rusty, that's too bad. He won't change his mind or anything, will he?"

"I don't think so. You want to ask him?"

"Heck no, not me! He's weird! Don't tell Tiffany I said that," he added hastily.

"Okay." Rusty was quiet then. He had always been part of Dan's birthday celebrations. Every single August since nursery school. "Dan, I'm sorry. But I promised him. Just this morning I said we'd be done on Friday."

"Yeah. Next year, then, okay?"

"Sure. Thanks. 'Bye." Rusty hung up. He squirted himself all over with mosquito spray and left the house in a hurry. They were earning a fortune on this job, he told himself, striding north on Grove. Seven weeks at fifty dollars a week was enough to pay for the basketball court, and the commissions would be gravy. Icing on the summer cake. Maybe I can get one of those red-white-and-blue nets, he thought. And a new basketball.

Wednesday and Thursday, whenever the sun wasn't too strong, Rusty and the yard crew worked on the old McFarland property, trying to change it into Smeltzer property.

"When I was a kid," Debbie said, "we always came here on Halloween for the caramel apples."

"Sure," Ruthann said, wielding a long pair of pruning shears. "I always"—snip, snip—"dumb shrubs anyway—had two costumes. So I could get two apples. Mrs. McFarland caught on one year, too, but she didn't say anything. Just winked at me."

"Wait'll I get back," Rusty told her, hurrying off to their dump in the woods at the rear of the property. He hated to miss any of Ruthann's stories.

The work was hardest on Thursday. Worried about finishing on time, they began early in the morning, and even though it was cooler, each hour seemed like two or three. Dan, his folks and his brother drove into the driveway at eleven to pick up Tiffany. Rusty watched Tiffany walk down the steps, dressed in palest pink, and thought maybe he had felt worse but he couldn't remember when. She got into the Browers' car, its tires crunched on the gravel, and then it was gone.

Rusty threw his rake into a pile of grass he'd been raking and walked off into the woods. He leaned up against a tree and looked at the giant brush pile they'd built over the past weeks. It showed how much work they'd done. If it caught on fire, he thought, these woods would go with it, leaving only a pile of ashes. All that would remain was their money in the bank.

"Big deal," he said out loud. He had more money now than he needed, if he counted what Mr. Smeltzer owed him. "Big deal," he said again. He slung the rake over his shoulder and headed back to the pile of grass.

11

The Payoff

Friday morning early, the work crew was on the job. They cleaned out the last small outbuilding and threw the trash onto their gigantic brush pile. Bob divided the paint into four buckets and they each took one side of the low building.

"While it dries, we can mow the front and back lawns," Rusty said, "and give it the second coat after lunch."

"The whole place looks real nice," Debbie called from the far side of the building. "The McFarlands ought to see it now that we fixed it all up."

"They can't see a thing. They're dead!" Ruth-ann hollered from her side.

"They can look down from heaven and see whatever they want," Debbie said determinedly. "I'll bet they're watching us right now."

"Oh yeah?" Ruthann slapped paint on the old wooden boards. "Well, maybe *Mrs.* McFarland's up there, but *he* isn't. He was a turkey, and he used to pinch his secretaries. Gramma told me."

Bob, Debbie and Rusty laughed. Ruthann knew the most interesting things. Rusty pictured white-haired little Mrs. McFarland passing out caramel apples to everyone in heaven, while far below her Mr. McFarland leered at the females assembled in hell.

While the first coat of paint dried, Bob and Ruthann mowed lawns. Rusty and Debbie edged the flower beds and yanked the persistent weeds. "It looks terrific," Debbie kept saying. "My folks drove by last night and they said it was a miracle. Dad thinks you're the greatest kid in our class. He said, 'That boy can work for me anytime.' Isn't that nice?"

"It sure is. Thanks."

"He'll tell everybody in the chair, too. You know how he is." Debbie laughed as she tossed thistles into the trash basket. Her father was the town dentist. Knowing that his patients couldn't talk with their mouths full of dental appliances, Dr. Purdy talked instead. Nonstop.

"Yeah," said Rusty, grinning in memory. "One time when he was cleaning my teeth, he told me about your summer at camp. He said one girl in your cabin came to camp with lice, so all summer you guys were itching and scratching, thinking she'd given everybody lice."

"He *would* tell that," she grumbled.

By three in the afternoon the work was finished. Rusty, Ruthann, Debbie and Bob stood on the front lawn and looked around, unable to believe they were done at last.

The three small outbuildings and barn glistened whitely, the shrubs around them tidy and green. The hedges stretched for a hundred yards down both sides of the property in a perfectly uniform line. All the many flower beds were weeded and the extra trees out back uprooted. New grass grew where the stumps had been. And inside, in the basement, boxes were neatly stacked at one end, while the walls and floor shone with fresh paint.

"Let's go get our money," Ruthann said.

"I told him we'd be here this afternoon. He has

the contracts for our first six weeks, and I'll finish this week's right now." Rusty pulled the paper from his back pocket and sat down on the porch steps to do the addition. "It averages out to fifty dollars a week for each of us. He owes each of us three hundred and fifty dollars! I guess it ought to look pretty good around here for that."

Ruthann was looking over his shoulder. "Hah!" she snorted. "Cheap at twice the price! If Smeltzer'd hired adults, it would have been twice as much. He's lucky."

"Yeah, come on," urged Debbie. "Ring the doorbell. We've waited long enough. I can get my kitty this evening if I get the check cashed."

"You're payin' three hundred and fifty bucks for a cat!" Bob was loudly scornful. "My second-hand tractor won't cost that much!"

"No, dumbo! The kitten's only seventy-five dollars, but I have to have cash. The lady said so. She lives on a farm north of town and she's got real pedigreed Burmese kittens."

"For *only* seventy-five bucks," Ruthann teased. "Debbie, are you sure your elevator goes to the top?" She tapped her head with one finger.

"Shut up, you guys," Debbie retorted comfortably. She ran up the steps and rang the doorbell.

The other three joined her in front of the door.

"Hi, Rusty," Tiffany said when she opened the door. "Hi, you guys. Is there something you want?"

"Yes. I told your dad we'd be here this afternoon to get paid. So here we are." Rusty felt the cool air from inside the house as it seeped out onto the porch.

"Daddy's on a business trip. Can you come back tomorrow?"

"Tomorrow?" Ruthann's tone was deadly. "He *knew* we were coming today. And we've waited all summer. Seven weeks!"

Tiffany looked stricken. "I'm sorry. But he'll be here in the morning. I know he will. And I'll tell him you're coming." She extended her hands in a helpless gesture. "I don't know what else to do."

"It's not your fault," Rusty said, seeing her face, wondering what it would be like to have to apologize for your father. "We'll be back in the morning. 'Bye."

Gloomily they collected their tools and set off for home, agreeing to meet on the Smeltzers' porch at nine on Saturday morning. "They like to sleep late," Debbie said. "Maybe that's too early."

"Tough beans," Rusty declared. He felt Ruthann's look, but she said nothing.

The next morning Rusty rang the Smeltzers' doorbell at nine o'clock. He rang it sharply, three times, just in case they were asleep.

"If you hadn't done it like that," Ruthann said, "I would have. My gramma's foaming at the mouth."

"So're my folks," the others agreed.

A long minute passed before the door opened. Mr. Smeltzer stood there in a maroon satin bathrobe. He was barefoot. "When you kids say morning, you mean morning." He frowned at the four of them on his doorstep. "Well, come in."

In the kitchen, Mr. Smeltzer sank into a chair by the table. "My flight was late. Didn't get in till after midnight. Let me just think where my checkbook is."

"Here's the list for this week's work," Rusty said, handing him the weekly contract. "It came out the same as all the others. You owe each of us three hundred and fifty dollars for the seven weeks."

Tiffany's father grunted as he rose from his chair. "That can't be right," he said as he went down the hallway toward the front of the house.

Behind him, the workers stared at one another, alarmed.

"I'll kill him," Ruthann muttered.

"He'll pay," insisted Rusty. "I've given him a contract every week and I have the copies. And my dad has seen them."

"Tell him that." Ruthann stood erect, arms folded.

Mr. Smeltzer reentered the kitchen, checkbook and pen in hand. "I can't seem to find those other contracts," he said, rubbing his forehead. "Probably too early in the morning. Why don't you kids come back later, when I've had a chance to get organized. Then we can go over all those contracts and check the work."

Rusty's face set in determined lines. He and his dad had had a talk the night before, and Rusty knew what had to be said.

"Mr. Smeltzer," Ruthann began venomously.

"Ruthann, let me." Rusty darted her a warning look as he took a step toward Mr. Smeltzer. "Sir, you've had seven weeks to go over those contracts. You've seen the work that's been done around here. And we've waited till the end to be paid. No adults would have waited, but we did, and we lost all the interest that money could've been earning. I told you last week that we'd be here Friday to pick up our money. And my dad has checked each contract as I brought it home. He said he'd be glad to come over here and discuss it with you if you want."

"I see," Mr. Smeltzer replied. He looked down at the most recent contract. "All those buildings have two coats of paint?"

"Yes, just like you ordered."

"And no weeds anywhere?"

"Not unless a sneaky one grew up overnight," Ruthann inserted, unable to be quiet any longer.

Bob and Debbie smiled at each other, then looked down at their feet.

"And you say you *each* earned three hundred and fifty dollars?"

"That's right. For seven weeks' work." Rusty looked at him directly.

"And wasn't there a bonus? We finished on time, before the party." Ruthann's eyes seemed bluer than ever now that she was tanned, and they challenged Mr. Smeltzer.

Tiffany's father coughed, then uncapped his pen. "I guess everything's in order, then." He swiftly wrote four checks, laying each one on the table in front of him. When he finished, he laid

the pen down on top of the checks. "Now, who's going to keep the place up? Mowing, weeding, the regular maintenance?"

Rusty looked at his crew. Each one in turn nodded slightly. He looked back at Mr. Smeltzer. "We will. The grass won't grow much in this heat, but we'll come back when we're needed."

"That'll be fine," he said heartily, appearing more cheerful now that the checks had been written and the awful deed was behind him. Rusty thought that the man hated to part with his money, but once it was done he seemed to accept the fact. "You kids work hard when you have to. Just like Tiffany and her piano practicing. Nothing beats determination, and I admire that." Now he could smile as he handed each of them a check.

Rusty winced inwardly and could hardly wait to get out of the house. Mr. Smeltzer was the most revolting person he had ever known. No wonder Tiffany was different. "Thank you very much," he said, peeking at his check. It was for $375.00. "And thanks for the tip."

On the sidewalk in front of the house, the crew compared checks. All were the same. "Nice tip," Bob said.

"Not even a buck a day," Ruthann observed. "He didn't bankrupt himself."

And then no one said anything. Rusty folded his check in half and pushed it deep into his jeans pocket. It was over, then, the big job. "Well, guess I'll go home and see what's happening," he said halfheartedly.

"I'm sorry we're done," Ruthann blurted. "I never had a summer like this." She started down the sidewalk, moving quickly.

"Hey?" Debbie called after her. "I'm going to get my kitten this afternoon. Wanta come with me?"

Ruthann turned. "I guess so. I mean, thanks."

"Come on. We can have lunch at my place and you can call your gramma."

Ruthann made a face. "Yeah. She's getting twitchy this summer. Drives me bats." She and Debbie fell into step, talking as they went toward Debbie's house.

Rusty and Bob watched them go. "I guess I'll go out to the quarry this afternoon," Bob said. "Wow all the girls with my nice white legs." He grimaced.

Rusty grinned. "Great idea. I'll see you there. Marty got our pool fixed, but it's still filling with water. You need a ride? My dad'll drive if I ask him." He began to look forward to the weekend. "I'll bike. See you there." Bob cranked up the motor on his mower and putted away as Rusty pulled the wagonload of tools toward home.

By Monday morning Rusty's legs were nearly as red as his hair, after two days of sun at the quarry with friends. He felt rich and rested and proud of himself. Timmons' Total Service had been one heck of an idea after all. Right the first time, he thought happily as he went downstairs for breakfast. The phone rang as he entered the kitchen.

"You get it," Julia said. She was pouring cereal into bowls.

"Timmons' Total Service," he answered. When he hung up he checked the job chart, then dialed Bob. "Hey, want to mow a lawn today?"

At the kitchen table, Julia shook her ponytail in amazement. "I'd never have believed it. I should have thought of a way to keep the Y.E.S. office open all summer."

"Yech!" Mike dumped several spoonfuls of sugar onto her cereal. "Summer's for *playing.* When's the pool going to be warm? Sara and I were having races before those dogs messed it all up!"

Julia pointed her spoon at Mike. "Don't whine, Mike. Just don't start my day like that, okay?"

"Geez! It took three calls just to get somebody to mow a lawn," Rusty complained as he joined his sisters at the table. "All of a sudden it's tough to find workers. I had this same trouble last night."

"Vacations are in August," Julia said. "And kids get tired of working. School starts in three weeks anyway."

"We just got out!" Rusty could never remember a faster summer. It had gone by like a jet.

"Nearly three months by the time we go back, and I'm ready to be a senior. Boy, am I ready," Julia announced.

The phone rang again, and Mike reached for her whistle. "Don't do it," Rusty warned her as he grabbed the phone.

The voice in his ear said, "Hi, Rusty. This is Jeremy."

"Is something wrong at Mrs. Sheffield's?"

"No. Everything's fine here. She likes me." He paused. "Doesn't Ruthann Miller have a job exercising a pony? An old circus pony?"

"Yeah, why?"

"Could you describe the pony?"

Rusty stopped lounging on the counter. "Sure, but why?"

"I'm sure I saw it going by here. I'm at Mrs. Sheffield's now."

"That's right. She exercises him early every morning." Jermy was so exasperating. Suddenly Rusty realized what he had really said. "You mean you saw the pony *alone*?"

"Yes. A saddle, but no rider."

"What'd he look like, what'd he look like?"

"Black-and-white. He had a black mane and tail, and he's big for a Shetland. He was throwing his head from side to side."

Rusty's stomach knotted. "That's him. That's Hitler." Why hadn't he insisted that someone else ride that horse? Why hadn't he been tougher with Ruthann? "Go look for her, Jermy," he managed to say. "The pony must've thrown her. Go look right away, okay?"

"Sure. He probably just dumped her in the grass somewhere over in the park. Try not to worry. We'll go now." The phone clicked in Rusty's ear.

"What's wrong, Rusty? You look awful." Julia

was standing next to him.

"Jermy saw Hitler. Saddle, but no rider. I think he threw her off somewhere. But where?" He headed for the back door. "Call Dad. Tell him I'm in the park. That's where she usually takes him for rides."

Julia ran after him down the sidewalk. "Rusty, maybe you're wrong. Maybe she's walking around town now trying to find the stupid horse."

Rusty wheeled his bike out of the garage. "No. If she was okay, she'd be with him. Something's wrong. I just *know* it."

12

The Pony's Trick

Rusty pedaled desperately across Grove and turned north toward the center of town. By now the knot in his stomach had clenched into a hard ball. She was down somewhere. He could feel it.

Ruthann Miller. From the beginning she had worked as hard as he had, and often longer. All through the steaming, itchy afternoons at the Smeltzers', when Bob and Debbie had complained, she had been able to joke. The manager in the blue suit with her hair pulled back in a bun. Rotten Ruthann, with the jutting chin and intense blue eyes, who saw life with absolute clarity.

When he passed Main and Center, he gave a

hurried glance down each street. But he knew she wouldn't be there. She'd said once that Hitler hated cars, and that was why she took him to the park. Or out by the caves.

Hampshire Park was in one direction, west on Parkview. The caves were east of town, near several farms. He'd have to decide which to try first. Then he remembered that Jermy had said he was at Mrs. Sheffield's when he saw Hitler. She lived on Parkview, only a few blocks from the park.

Rusty shot his left arm out to signal a left turn and flew down Parkview toward Hampshire Park. He raced under its stone arch entrance, the bike tires spraying gravel as he hit the path. Way ahead he saw two figures on foot. He could ask them to look. The more people looking, the better.

As he drew near he recognized Jermy and Mrs. Sheffield. But no Ruthann. "You see anything?" he asked as he roared up beside them.

"Not yet. We did the area around the shelter house and the baby swings. Now we're going to the picnic tables and that woodsy part," Jermy said solemnly, pointing to the woods.

"I'll go over by the boathouse and the lake. If

you see my dad, tell him I'm over there, okay?"

"Be careful, Russell," scolded Mrs. Sheffield. "And don't ride so fast."

Rusty wheeled around and headed for the lake, ignoring Mrs. Sheffield's advice. He had to ride fast. Ruthann needed help.

He stopped at the boathouse, hoping Mr. Thompson had seen her or the pony. Automatically he checked the pail by the door. A clean pail meant no Mr. Thompson, and tobacco spittle meant he was on duty. The pail that morning was clean, and Rusty got back on his bike. He had counted on Mr. Thompson to have seen something. *Anything.*

He began a careful quartering of the areas around the lakeshore where the land formed dips and hollows. It would be easy for a body to lie unseen in tall weeds or clumps of grass. Especially someone as thin as she is, he thought.

Rusty remembered what Jermy had said. *Probably just dumped her in the grass somewhere over in the park.* He was trying to make me feel better, Rusty thought.

You're too nice, Rusty. Just let ol' Rotten handle it the next time. Things she had said to him came back. But she was wrong. He wasn't nice.

Or tough, either. He just sounded tough sometimes, and there was a difference. Anyone tough
would have kept her away from that pony. Anyone nice wouldn't have taken money from the
pony job.

"Nothing yet?" called a voice.

He looked up to see his father, tie and suit coat
off, running toward him. Around his neck
bounced the blue cord and Mike's police whistle.

"Why've you got the whistle?" Rusty got off his
bike.

Mr. Timmons smiled encouragingly. "It's how
I'm going to tell the town we've found Ruthann.
The police gave them out to several searchers,
and Mike gave me hers. Whole town's looking
for her, Rusty. It's only a matter of time."

Rusty tried to smile back at his dad, who
sounded so confident. "Thanks." He turned away
and resumed on foot his systematic search of the
lake area.

Mr. Timmons said, "Don't worry. We'll find
her." And then he was off and running in a different direction from Rusty.

And how will we find her? Rusty asked himself. Into his mind flashed a gory picture of
Ruthann on the ground, trampled by horse's

hooves. Blood all over her clothes—blood on her face and matted in her hair. *Red, red.* The color she loved. Appalled by his own imagination, he began to run, calling, "Ruthann? Ruthann? It's me, Rusty! *Ruthann!*"

He glimpsed something in the distance and ran to see, just in case. It was then that he found her. She was way down by the edge of the lake, one foot in the water. The lake lapped gently to and fro—now on her foot, now pulled back on itself. She was perfectly still, the sunlit hair spread out on the gray pebbles of the rocky beach. Her blouse was what was red, and there wasn't any blood after all.

Rusty bent over her, afraid. Afraid of the stillness of her. "Ruthann?" One of her arms was across her waist. He touched it. "Ruthann?" The ball of pain filled his throat now, and he couldn't say any more.

"Rusty? Son?" He felt his father's hand on his shoulder. "Let me feel for a pulse." Mr. Timmons put his fingers on Ruthann's neck. He closed his eyes and bowed his head as he moved his fingers, searching for a pulse.

"Thank the Lord," he breathed. "It's weak, but it's there. Don't move her, Russ. Just hold on to

her hand. I'll get the ambulance." He rose from his knees. "Talk to her. Let her know we're here. Keep talking to her." He turned, running toward the park entrance.

FWEEEP! FWEEEEEEP! FWEEEEP! The piercing whistle announced their discovery.

Rusty sat down on the stony beach and held tight to her hand, which was limp and cool, and not at all like her. He saw how tanned the hand was, its fingernails broken from the summer's work.

Rusty felt summer tumble down around him like the fragile sand cities he had built at Lake Cumberland. Without Ruthann, Timmons' Total Service would have been plain hard work. With her, it had been a success . . . and fun. She could still make him furious, but she'd stopped doing that on purpose. They were comfortable with each other. He knew how she thought.

"Ruthann," he said, "it's *me* who's rotten. Not you." He bent over her hand, and the tears ran slowly down his face. "I don't care about the dumb old basketball court. You should've told me more about Hitler. If it'd been Dan, he'd have told me. He'd have said he wouldn't do it, or something."

Rusty saw his tears drop on her blouse, making wet blotches on the red material. Ruthann never stirred. If she dies, he thought, how could I ever forget? It's all my fault.

When the ambulance came, Mr. Timmons jumped out first. Rusty watched as he helped the two first-aid squad people slide Ruthann onto a stretcher. "I'll ride with her," Rusty said. "I can keep talking to her."

He walked beside Ruthann's stretcher, holding her hand as she was carried into a hospital in downtown Cincinnati. Mr. Timmons had agreed with the ambulance driver that the services of a big city hospital might be needed.

"Put her in here," said a young woman in a white coat. Her badge said "Dr. Steinbrenner." "We got your call, and a neurosurgeon plus two other specialists are on their way. I'll stay with her now. You can all wait in the waiting room."

"No," said Rusty.

"Come on, son." His dad put his hand on Rusty's shoulder.

"I'm not leaving her." He thought his face was probably all messed up. People could tell he'd been crying.

"It's a hospital rule," Dr. Steinbrenner said gently. "I won't leave her alone. I promise. I'll come get you the minute I can."

"Come on, Russ," his dad said again. He took Rusty's hand just as he had when Rusty was a little boy, and pulled him away from Ruthann's stretcher. He let himself be pulled away. He could tell he didn't stand a chance against the rules. They wouldn't understand. Rules never did.

Out in the emergency waiting room, Rusty sat on the black vinyl couch nearest the door. Maybe he could hear what the doctors were saying when they examined her. Or if she cried out, if they hurt her, he could run back in.

"How about a can of pop?" Mr. Timmons suggested.

"No, thanks." Rusty looked at his hands. "How long do you think it'll be?"

"Could be a long time. And I'll have to make some calls. Your mother doesn't know we're here, or Julia, and I should call Ruthann's house immediately."

Rusty looked up. "Yeah, her gramma. I hope she knows where to call Ruthann's mother. She works somewhere here in the city."

His father shook his head. "I don't know about that. Anyway, I'll be as quick as I can. I'll use a phone in the main lobby." He squeezed Rusty's shoulder and was gone.

Rusty sank back into the couch and waited. The pain in his stomach had subsided into a dull, hard ache. And now there was nothing he could do to help Ruthann. The time to have done that was early in the summer, when she had taken the pony job. When he had thought there'd be trouble, but didn't really find out. Didn't *want* to know for sure. And all along his parents had warned him about dangerous jobs.

Over and over he tortured himself with the same thoughts. He couldn't seem to stop. Nor could he make himself think anything good.

"Everyone's on the way here. Rusty, are you sure I can't get you anything?" Mr. Timmons took Rusty's chin and raised his face so that they looked at each other.

"It's all my fault," he said, needing to say it out loud. And then he was crying again and his dad was holding him. "It's all my fault. I knew that was a bad horse, and I let her ride him anyway."

"I was afraid that's what you were thinking," his dad said. He held Rusty close and talked right into his ear. "But you're wrong, Russ, you're wrong. Ruthann's her own person. She would have ridden that pony no matter what. Think about that for a minute and you'll see the truth of it."

"But I should've stopped her! Somehow. Only she always . . . she always said it was nothing. Or she changed the subject." He pulled away and sat up straight. "That's what she did. She always talked about something else. And I let it go. I let her do it, even when I knew." He leaned against his father and breathed raggedly, trying not to cry. You wouldn't catch *her* in any waiting room blubbering like a baby.

Rusty felt a hand touch his hair and looked up to see Dr. Steinbrenner. She was bending over to talk to him. "Her pulse is stronger now. And the doctors are with her. She looks like a pretty strong girl to me—what do you think?"

Rusty sat up, wiping at his face, surprised that a stranger should see so much so fast. "She's strong, yeah. She's very tough."

"I have a few minutes," she said, pushing her stethoscope down into the white pocket of her jacket. "Let me show you our coffee shop."

"No. I better stay here. Ruthann might need

me." Rusty settled again into the black couch.

The doctor cocked her head to one side. "I wish I had such a good friend. But she may need you more later, to talk to her and cheer her up. You can't do that without a bite of food sometime."

"She's right, son. This room is depressing." Mr. Timmons stood up.

"No," Rusty said. This time he wasn't going to budge.

"Is there someone here named Rusty?" A tall, balding man in a white coat looked around the door to the waiting room.

"Me! I'm Rusty!" He bounded off the couch.

"You can come in, then, but only for a few minutes." The man frowned. "And don't say anything to upset her. It's just that we can't get her to be quiet until she's seen you."

"Okay. Sure, sure." So she was giving the doctors a hard time! That was wonderful.

In seconds, he was looking down at her lying on a tall, narrow cart with wheels. An I.V. bottle on a stand stood next to the cart, and he assumed it was dripping good stuff into her arm. All but her head was covered with a white sheet, and her eyelids were closed. She was completely still.

"Hey, Ruthann?"

The eyelids drifted upward. "Tell Dan . . ." She closed her eyes briefly and opened them again. "Tell Dan he can have the pony job." She gave a fleeting smile before her forehead wrinkled in pain.

Rusty wanted to laugh, and shout, and kick a hole in a drum. If he'd had Mike's whistle, he'd have blown it a hundred times. Not there, of course, that'd probably hurt Ruthann's head. Unconscious for who knew how long? And then wake up and say, "Tell Dan he can have the pony job"?

She was going to be all right. He could feel it. "Okay, I'll tell him. If I ever see him." Rusty found he couldn't say all the things he wanted to say. "I'll come back. Whenever you want. I won't leave."

"That'd be great." An expression of pain settled on her face, and she was quiet.

"All right, Ruthann. Now, if we let him in again later, you have to promise you'll be quiet and rest. Is that a deal?" The bald doctor had moved next to Rusty and was bending over her. When he spoke to Ruthann, his voice was comforting.

"Deal," she whispered.

Rusty gave her a long look. Then he was content to go back out to the waiting room with the doctor. There they found Rusty's mother, Ruthann's grandmother, a woman Rusty didn't know and Dan, too.

"Did you see her? Is she all right? Can I go in now?" The woman Rusty didn't know spoke first. He supposed it was Barbara Miller, Ruthann's mother. Everything about her was thin. Thin hair, thin face, painfully thin body. Her eyes were blue, like Ruthann's, only faded in color and sunk deep in her face. She looked terrified.

"You her mother?" Rusty spoke before the doctor had a chance.

"Yes, is she all right?"

Both Rusty and the doctor nodded, and the doctor spoke. "We hope so, but she has a bad concussion plus a broken collarbone. I'm putting her in our intensive care unit for a time. May I talk with you privately?" He and Ruthann's mother walked to a corner of the waiting room.

"What're they saying?" Rusty asked worriedly.

"Probably 'Who's going to pay for this?'" Dan told Rusty. "Not anything bad." He smiled reassuringly. "I was at your place with Marty. We got the chemicals adjusted in the pool, and it's already warm. Your mom said it was okay if I came along to keep you company."

Gramma Miller and Mrs. Timmons joined them. "Does she look okay to you?" Gramma Miller asked Rusty. The old woman's eyes were wet and she was shaking.

"She looks fine . . . and talks fine, too. Dan," he added, grinning, "she said you could have the pony job."

"I deserved that," Dan said, shrugging his shoulders. He smiled at Rusty.

"Don't you go near that horse," Gramma warned in a quivery voice. She sat down on the couch. "I intend to see that no one in Hampshire has anything to do with that animal." Her voice grew stronger with each word.

"Count me in on that committee," Mrs. Timmons said.

13

Rainbow

It was the last Sunday in August, the day before school was to begin, when the Timmons family was able to give Ruthann a homecoming party. She had been home from the hospital for two weeks and was slowly getting well. Her celebration was a pool party and barbecue. Dan had been invited and Tiffany, too—something Mrs. Timmons had insisted on.

"It won't make you any less happy to have her here. I think you kids never gave her a chance. She's so different from all of you that you just crossed her off at the beginning."

"She's different all right," Rusty said. He couldn't believe that his mother understood so little about Tiffany. He plopped a pile of napkins on a tray beside the hot-dog roasting forks.

By four in the afternoon, everyone had arrived. Gramma Miller came down the sidewalk carrying an enormous chocolate cake. Ruthann was beside her, paler and even thinner, but looking like her old self.

"I'm sorry, Mrs. Timmons, but my mother couldn't make it," Ruthann apologized when everyone had gathered in the kitchen. She looked around at the group. "Hi, Julie. Greg. Hi, Dan." Surprise colored her voice. "I heard you came to the hospital that first day. And thanks for the Garfield book." She laughed. "I haven't ever been famous before, but I like it. I've got *piles* of cards and presents."

"And plants," Gramma Miller said appreciatively. "We look like a florist's shop."

Tiffany stepped forward. Both she and Mr. Timmons had been standing near the door to the backyard. "And did you get my rainbow? We sent it to Christ Hospital, but I wasn't sure it would find you."

"*You* sent it? There wasn't any card. Nobody knew." She moved forward a bit in Tiffany's direction. "It's the most beautiful thing I've ever had. The nurse put it in my window and I watched it every day. Remember, Rusty? When you came to visit me, I said I always looked for it first thing in the morning?"

"Yeah . . . the big dangly thing that threw colors around the room. It's pretty," he added politely. This was going okay. Maybe his mother wasn't completely crazy.

"Now it's in my room at home," Ruthann told Tiffany.

"Let's go out by the pool," Mrs. Timmons suggested. "The invalid needs sunshine for her tan and that gorgeous hair." She winked at Ruthann.

"Yeah," Ruthann said, delight in her voice. "Before, I was a whole beige person. Blah hair, blah skin. Like a camel. What am I going to *do* this winter?"

"Dye it," Julia said firmly. *"We'll* never tell. Let's go out now before all the ice melts in the lemonade."

FWEEEEEP! FWEEEEEP! Mike bounced down the steps from upstairs and into the kitchen.

Mr. Timmons held the door open for Gramma and scolded Mike at the same time. "Now don't blow that thing again!"

"But that's a happy blow. A party blow. Doesn't it make you feel good?" Mike looked from one person to another.

"Yes," Tiffany said. "I like it. Where'd you get it?"

"I can't go in the pool," Ruthann told Rusty later when the picnic supper was over. Dan and Tiffany, Julia and Greg, Mike and her friend Sara and Rusty's parents were sitting around the pool. She and Rusty were in lawn chairs, as was Gramma Miller. "I can't help with the job service either, so it's a good thing you're closing it down before school starts. And I can only go half days the first week. You name it, and I can't do it. That doctor is tough."

"Yes, and if you don't mind him, I'll take a switch to you, young lady." Gramma Miller sounded loving, but firmer than usual.

"Is she getting mean?" Rusty grinned at them.

"Yeah, terrible mean. She makes me go to bed at ten o'clock, too, just when all the good movies start."

Rusty admitted, "I always go to bed then." He was quiet awhile. "Ruthann, why do you think Hitler threw you? Why'd he keep on doing that?"

She shrugged. "Who knows? Why'd my mom leave home?"

"Ruthann!" Gramma Miller was aghast.

"Gramma, it's no secret. Everybody knows."

Rusty looked away, embarrassed.

Ruthann's voice was matter-of-fact as she continued. "That old pony never liked anybody, near's I can tell. Probably Mr. Langendorfer's brother could handle him, and he was the only one, and that's why the circus didn't keep him. But I tried and couldn't do it. Maybe the pony just can't help it. I hear Mr. Langendorfer sold him, too. Anyway, I'm never *ever* going to ride old circus ponies again. Not even for five dollars a minute."

"Yeah, that was dumb of me. Really dumb." Rusty looked down at his lap.

"Oh no you don't. You can't take away my dumb." She tossed her hair back in a practiced motion. "That's *my* dumb and you can't have it."

"Okay. You win for now. But when you get better, watch out."

"That's fair." She gazed at the pool, where the rest of her party were enjoying themselves in the water. "You ever teach anybody how to swim?"

"I taught Mike. I told you that."

"Oh, yeah, well . . . I'm afraid of the water on my head."

Rusty understood what she had really said.

"You have enough money for a car yet?" she asked abruptly. "Debbie told me you'd be the first one in our class to get a car."

"Nah, I just said that. I was really saving for a basketball court, a real one like at school. Right out there." Rusty pointed to the spot at the end of their driveway where he had envisioned the court for so many weeks.

"Basketball? I didn't know you played basketball."

"It'd be something different, you know? Hardly anybody in our class has a basketball court at their house."

Again, she looked toward the pool. "Dan's really good at basketball, isn't he?"

"The best. And I'm not such a bad guard."

Ruthann nodded. "So why don't you get it? It can't take very long to put one up. And you've got plenty of money."

"I don't know." He forced himself to go on. "I thought we could pay the hospital or the doctor with the money the Service made. A lot of it came from you anyhow."

This time Ruthann didn't have a quick answer. When she spoke, her voice was quiet. "Mr. Langendorfer's taking care of all that, with insurance. And I like basketball, too. If you had a court here, Dan could come, and Debbie. She's on the JV team. We could have games right here in the neighborhood, and maybe *I'd* make the girls' team this year—with Debbie."

"Okay. If you're sure. But Dan'd probably want Tiffany here."

"That's okay. She can keep score or something. Hurry up and order it."

"I can do it tomorrow after school. Got any more bright ideas?"

"Sure. But not right now. I'll let you know."

He smiled at her, certain that she would. He could count on Ruthann.